"You can go out the back to avoid the reporters."

"Won't do any good." She'd only just realized this part. "My car is out front."

Her vanity plate read PAPRGRL. Everyone knew who drove that car.

"All right. You can stay back here but stick to that sink over there like it's your long-lost best friend. Do not move from that spot."

"I won't."

He reached for the door, the move putting his face so very close to hers.

"As long as you give me an exclusive sound bite," she added.

He turned, looked directly at her, practically nose to nose. "I'll give you whatever you want, Rey. I always have."

And then he was gone.

She leaned against the wall, had to wait until her heart stopped pounding before she moved.

She was not, *was not* going to get tangled up with Colt Tanner again.

Never, ever, ever.

IN SELF DEFENSE

USA TODAY Bestselling Author

DEBRA WEBB

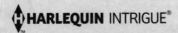
HARLEQUIN INTRIGUE®

Franklin County, Tennessee, has a large community of Mennonites. During the years we lived in Tennessee we were pleased to call so many of them friends. This book is dedicated to all the folks who embrace and appreciate what makes each of us unique.

ISBN-13: 978-1-335-64064-2

In Self Defense

PLEASE RECYCLE

THIS PRODUCT IS RECYCLABLE

Recycling programs for this product may not exist in your area.

Printed in U.S.A.

HARLEQUIN®

™ www.Harlequin.com

Debra Webb is the award-winning *USA TODAY* bestselling author of more than one hundred novels, including those in reader-favorite series Faces of Evil, the Colby Agency and the Shades of Death. With more than four million books sold in numerous languages and countries, Debra's love of storytelling goes back to childhood on a farm in Alabama. Visit Debra at www.debrawebb.com.

Books by Debra Webb

Visit the Author Profile page at Harlequin.com.

CAST OF CHARACTERS

Audrey Anderson—Celebrated investigative journalist who comes home to take over the family newspaper.

Sheriff Colton Tanner—He broke Audrey's heart in high school, and he would do most anything to make things right between them.

Sarah Sauder—There's a dead man in her kitchen. Could this young Mennonite wife and mother have shot and killed him, or is she covering for someone else?

Wesley Sauder—Sarah's husband is oddly absent when his wife needs him most. What is he hiding from?

Burt Johnston—Franklin County coroner.

Brian Peterson—Audrey's lifelong friend and the editor at the newspaper.

Chapter One

The red and blue lights flashed in the night.

Audrey Anderson opened her car door and stepped out onto the gravel road. She grimaced and wished she'd taken time to change her shoes, but time was not an available luxury when the police scanner spit out the code for a shooting that ended in a call to the coroner. Good thing her dedicated editor, Brian Peterson, had his ear to the police radio pretty much 24/7 and immediately texted her.

The sheriff's truck was already on-site, along with two county cruisers and the coroner's van. So far no news vans and no cars that she noticed belonging to other reporters from the tri-county area. Strange, that cocky reporter from the *Tullahoma Telegraph* almost always arrived on the scene before Audrey. Maybe she had a friend in the department.

Then again, Audrey had her own sources, too. She reached back into the car for her bag. So far the closest private source she had was the sheriff himself—which was only because he still felt guilty for cheating on her back in high school.

Audrey was not above using that guilt whenever the need arose.

Tonight seemed like the perfect time to remind the man she'd once thought she would marry that he owed her one or two or a hundred.

She shuddered as the cold night air sent a shiver through her. Late February was marked by all sorts of lovely blooms and promises of spring, but it was all just an illusion. It was still winter and Mother Nature loved letting folks know who was boss. Like tonight—the gorgeous sixty-two-degree sunny day had turned into a bone-chilling evening. Audrey shivered, wishing she'd worn a coat to dinner.

Buncombe Road snaked through a farming community situated about halfway between Huntland and Winchester—every agricultural mile fell under the Franklin County Sheriff's jurisdiction. The houses, mostly farmhouses sitting amid dozens if not hundreds of acres of pastures and fields, were scattered few and far between. But that wasn't the surprising part of the location. *This* particular house and farm belonged to a Mennonite family. Rarely did violence or any other sort of trouble within this quiet, closed community ripple beyond its boundaries. Most issues were handled privately and silently. The Mennonites kept to themselves for the most part and never bothered anyone. A few operated public businesses within the local community, and most interactions were kept strictly within the business domain. There was no real intermingling or socializing within the larger community—not even Winchester, which was the county seat and buzzed with activity.

Whatever happened inside this turn-of-the-nineteenth-century farmhouse tonight was beyond the closed community's ability to settle amid their own ranks.

Though Audrey had lived in Washington, DC, for the past ten years, she had grown up in this part of southern Tennessee. There had never been a murder among the Mennonites that she could recall. In fact, she was reasonably certain there had never been any violence involving one of them, unless the perpetrator was someone who had abandoned the Mennonite life. Even that was nearly unheard of.

Tucking her clutch bag under her arm, Audrey palmed her cell phone and shoved the car door shut with her hip. The four-inch heels she had chosen to wear to the Chamber of Commerce Business Awards Banquet dug into the gravel with each step she made. She sighed. Sacrifices were a part of getting the story. What was the loss of a pair of shoes if there was a nice spike in subscriptions?

For a newspaper, circulation—whether print or online—was everything.

She might be the owner, but she also had the most investigative experience, which meant she had to get out in the field—had to get her hands dirty. How else was she going to turn the *Winchester Gazette* around? She not only had to get the story, she had to uncover the story no one else unearthed. It helped considerably that her family had deep roots in Franklin County, knew God and everyone who lived within a fifty-mile radius of her hometown. More important, the sitting sheriff—his white cowboy hat came into view even as she thought of him—really did owe her.

He owed her big-time, and she intended to see that he never forgot.

She reached for the yellow crime scene tape draped from bare crepe myrtle to crepe myrtle along the front of the yard, raised it and ducked under it. As if he'd sensed the interloper at his crime scene, Sheriff Colton Tanner turned to watch her stride up the driveway, the headlights from the cluster of vehicles illuminating her path.

It wasn't necessary to see his eyes to know his gaze roamed from the top of her blond head down the peach-colored silk blouse and classic broomstick skirt she wore all the way to the sleek matching high heels that would be ruined after this outing. As if to confirm her assumption, he shook his head and cut off the deputy who had headed Audrey's way, no doubt to inform her that she needed to stay outside the yellow tape perimeter.

Colt double-timed it down the steps and strode toward her. "Rey, you know you cannot be here."

Rey. From the day she was brought home from the hospital everyone around here had called her Rey. That was the way of things in the South. Your name was either chopped in half for a nickname or you were called by both your first and middle. No one seemed capable of simply using a person's given name.

"You have a body," Audrey announced, one hand on her cocked hip as she peered up at the man who had shattered her naive heart at the ripe old age of seventeen. "I have a newspaper. Alone, neither one is particularly noteworthy. But the story of what actually happened can mean the difference between merely dead and murdered and, in the case of my newspaper, staying in business or going bankrupt. So, like you, Sheriff, I'm here for the story either way."

His gray eyes filled with confusion that quickly

morphed into sympathy. Audrey wanted to shake him and tell him she didn't need his pity. She just needed the story. The old saying "if it bleeds, it leads" was far too true. Except right now she would take sympathy or whatever else it took to get the story. She was just as ruthless as any other reporter.

"Well." He heaved out a breath and braced his hands on his lean hips, matching her stance. "Be that as it may, this is a crime scene, Rey. Police business."

He shrugged those broad shoulders and flared his wide hands. Why oh why had she noticed his lean hips or his long legs or his broad shoulders? Or any of those other utterly masculine assets before recovering control of her wayward thoughts? Dear God, she was hopeless. Or maybe simply desperate. She'd been back in Winchester for over six months and she hadn't had a single date. Hadn't had one for as many months or more before the big move. Quite possibly the only thing wrong with her was nothing more than basic human need.

Whatever the case, she would not be fulfilling that need with this gorgeous cowboy. Not now or ever. They were over. All she needed was information and perhaps a look at the crime scene.

"I'm a reporter," she argued. "I have an obligation to keep the community informed."

"I understand that." He raised a hand before she could interrupt his rebuttal. "But you can't go showing up like this and crossing the perimeter—"

"Please." She reached into her bag and retrieved disposable gloves. "I know my way around a crime scene better than a single one of your deputies. I daresay," she added as she met his weary gaze, "better than you."

Audrey started forward once more. Her destination was the porch. Once she was on the porch she would pull on protective footwear and go right on inside. The door was open. The body was in there and most likely so was the person who pulled the trigger.

"All that research you've done as a big-city crime reporter is not impressing me here," he protested, catching up to her after hesitating five or so seconds—no doubt just so he could watch her walk away. Some things never changed. "This is official police business, Rey. As much as I'd like to do you a favor, you cannot go in there."

She stopped at the bottom of the wooden porch steps. "Are you saying you don't trust me, Colt?"

The pained expression that pinched his handsome face gave her immense pleasure. It really was bad form to enjoy a little payback after all these years, but no one was perfect. When it came to Colt, she knew exactly which buttons to push. Though she'd only been back home for six months, she'd deduced very quickly where she stood with anyone important to her goal of saving the family newspaper. The sheriff was in the top five of that short list. Thankfully, their shared history made him a little easier to handle.

"Rey, you know that's not it. We have official procedures about this sort of thing. I let you in there, evidence could be considered contaminated and my case would be jeopardized."

She sighed as if the idea hadn't once occurred to her. Rules of evidence, something else she knew very, very well. "Then tell me what's going on and I'll be more than happy to get out of your way."

He issued another of those frustrated exhales as he glanced across the yard at the deputy who was supposed to be guarding the perimeter. Audrey suspected the poor guy was in for a dressing-down. Truth was, Colt didn't have even one deputy who would deny her entrance onto any crime scene. Of course, this was the first shooting since she'd taken over the paper.

Not just a shooting; there was a deceased victim. Possibly a homicide.

"Sarah Sauder—she's Melvin Yoder's daughter," Colt said with just enough reluctance to remind her she had forced him to make this confession, "shot and killed a man who broke into her house."

"A robbery attempt?" The idea didn't make a whole lot of sense considering the Mennonites weren't exactly known for keeping valuable items that might be easily pawned or readily sold lying around the house.

Colt shrugged. "We don't know anything yet. Burt's having a look at the body now. You understand that part takes time. It might be a while before the body can be moved, and we're collecting evidence in there." He gestured toward the house as if she might not be following all he'd told her. "Maybe by noon or so tomorrow we'll have some idea what happened here tonight."

Burt Johnston was the county coroner and nearing eighty. Audrey seriously doubted he would take a minute longer than necessary, especially at this hour. Considering his age, getting a call at this time of night wouldn't be something that prompted him to dally. As for the evidence, she had no intention of waiting for forensic reports. Absolutely not. Her goal was to splash this story on the front page of tomorrow morning's edition.

"Why the delay in moving the body?" Usually the police liked getting the body out of the way once the scene was properly photographed and drawn. No need to keep the deceased—the key piece of evidence that deteriorated every second it remained at room temperature or exposed to the elements—amid the fray of fully processing a scene.

"We've got a call into Branch. We want him to have a look at the dead guy—the victim—before we do anything else."

And now they arrived at the meat of the situation. Branch Holloway was a US marshal. Well, well, this wasn't just any dead guy—this was a dead guy with some connection to the Feds. Maybe an escaped prisoner from one of Tennessee's federal prisons. Or a fugitive from the most-wanted list. Her mind ticked off the numerous possibilities that would require the involvement of the Marshals Service.

She asked, "What's the connection to the Sauders?"

Colt removed his hat and plowed his fingers through his hair, the tension in the set of his shoulders warning that he was losing his patience with her. "Sarah says she's never seen him before. She woke up from a dead sleep, heard someone downstairs and did what she had to do to protect her family."

Skeptical, Audrey asked, "Where's her husband?"

"He's on his way home. He was out of town. One of my deputies is inside with Sarah and her kids."

"Did you ID the victim?"

A truck pulled into the yard alongside the sheriff's. Big black crew cab with four-wheel drive. *Branch Holloway.*

Colt touched her arm. "I'm gonna need you to step back outside that yellow tape, Rey."

Now that Branch was here, Colt had to go all cocky and by the book. Colt and Branch had been rivals since high school. Showing up your high school nemesis trumped giving a tip to the girl whose heart you broke any day of the week or, in this case, night.

"Anything else about this incident I can run in tomorrow's edition?" She wasn't leaving without something more—at least not willingly.

"Colt, what's going on?" Branch removed his black Stetson as he approached. He gave her a nod. "Rey."

"Marshal." She returned his nod and smiled as if she'd been waiting all night for him to appear.

When she'd left home headed to college, one of the few things that had stuck with Audrey was the image of Branch Holloway. Back then he'd been a star quarterback for the Tennessee Volunteers. He'd graduated a couple of years before Colt and her. Like Colt, the man was the quintessential cowboy. She and her best friend Sasha had harbored secret crushes on Branch Holloway. His college football career had made him a real-life celebrity right here in Winchester.

Why couldn't she have fallen in love with this cowboy?

But she hadn't, and however much she'd lusted after Branch, her gaze shifted to Colt. Way back in eighth grade she'd promised to marry Colton Tanner as soon as they both graduated from college. They'd been boyfriend and girlfriend from seventh grade until he cheated on her with her archnemesis near the end of senior year. A blast of fury burned through her even now. She'd wasted all that time only to have her heart shattered. As if she'd telegraphed those thoughts to the man responsible for all her pain, Colt met her glare, and she could see the regret in his gray eyes.

Colt Tanner and Branch Holloway had been the hottest, most popular guys in school. Colt had the coal-black hair and pale gray eyes. Branch was blond with gold eyes. He and Branch were both tall and athletic; still were nearly two decades later. Both had been hometown heroes. Except Colt was a cheater. Damn him.

"Well, I'll let you gentlemen get back to business."

Both tipped their hats at her and bid a good night like true Southern gentlemen.

Audrey turned and marched to the end of the sidewalk and then back down the gravel drive, cringing with each slide of a leather heel between the crushed rocks. She would snap a few photos and hurry back to the paper to update the front page. The Future Farmers of America's upcoming annual pig-catching contest would have to be moved to page two.

By the time she found the perfect angle for a photo of the house and the crime scene tape, Colt and Branch had gone into the house. Audrey took a few more shots with her cell phone and headed to her car.

"Hey there, Miss Anderson."

She hesitated as she reached for the door. Deputy Calvin Stevens grinned at her.

"I guess the full moon brought out the crazies tonight," he said.

"Guess so." She leaned against the door and waited as he came closer. Cal was a big flirt. If he'd been inside the house she might be able to get a little more for her story. She glanced around. How odd that no other reporters had shown up yet. "But it looks like I'm the only one who arrived to watch all the fun," she teased, scanning the road in both directions. "I haven't seen another reporter."

"Sarah Sauder's daddy called the sheriff direct and the sheriff called the coroner. They wanted to keep this quiet." Cal grinned. "I figured the sheriff called you personally."

Well, well. So how did Brian hear about this? Maybe he was the one with the real source in the sheriff's department. "I'll never tell," she said with a wink.

"You probably saw this kind of thing all the time in the big city." Cal gave her a look that said he'd made it his business to learn a whole lot of things about her. "I heard about all those awards you won." The deputy leaned against her car, close enough for her to smell his freshly applied after-shave. Did he keep a bottle in the glove box of his county cruiser?

"I spent a lot of time in the field." The statement wasn't really an answer to his question, but she suspected he wouldn't notice. He was making conversation with the newest single lady in town. A small-town tradition.

"The sheriff says you trained with cops all over the country."

Only a slight exaggeration, taken directly from the bio on her website. "Wherever the story took me, I immersed myself in the community, including law enforcement."

Cal chuckled. "Is it true you helped to capture a serial rapist?"

"I did." The story had won her the esteemed Courage in Journalism Award. "I was following up on a victim who had survived an attack by the elusive killer when he came back to finish what he'd started."

Audrey had connected with the victim. She'd

felt at ease talking to Audrey when she didn't feel comfortable talking to the police. The younger woman had called, said she felt like someone had been watching her for a couple of days. Audrey had urged her to call the police but she refused. What else was there to do but go over to her house and try to help? Still, she had no intention of becoming a victim herself. En route she'd called the detective assigned to the case and let him know what was happening.

By the time she arrived, the rapist was already in the house with the victim. Audrey grabbed her courage with both hands, walked in and distracted him until the cops showed up. Looking back, walking into that house knowing the guy was inside was foolhardy, but she hadn't really had a choice.

"You are one cool lady, Miss Anderson."

"Why thank you, Cal. You should call me Rey. Everybody does."

He shrugged. "All right. *Rey.*"

"It's hard to believe this guy broke into Sarah's house." She made the statement as if she was personal friends with Sarah Sauder and she knew all about the dead guy.

"For sure." Cal glanced at the house, then checked in both directions to ensure no one was nearby. "Especially considering he came all the way from Chicago to do it. Sarah swears she never laid eyes on the guy before. Kind of hard to believe considering he came this far."

Chicago. Interesting. Audrey nodded. "Just totally crazy, isn't it?"

"Oh yes, ma'am. Sheriff Tanner no sooner ran the man's name than some detective from up there called and wanted to know what was going on."

"So this guy has a record?" It was possible someone from Chicago was attempting to horn his way into the local drug trade—not that there was much of a problem in the Winchester area, but most towns had at least some drug issues. Still, why break into a Mennonite woman's house? Unless, being from Chicago, he lost his bearings and broke into the wrong house. To an outsider, the roads around here all looked alike. At night, they all looked alike even to Audrey. Not so surprising, considering she had lived everywhere but here since she left for college.

"Oh yeah. Big-time. That big-city detective said the guy has ties to the mob."

So that was why Colt had called in Branch. Branch's first assignment with the Marshals Service was in Chicago. He likely knew all about Chicagoland crime families. This potential breaking-and-entering had just shifted to something else entirely.

"Do you know his name?"

Cal shook his head. "He's a big guy, though.

With red hair. She got him square in the chest with her husband's deer-hunting rifle. One shot. He was probably dead before he hit the floor."

"I'm glad she and the children weren't harmed."

Before Cal could say more, the front door of the house opened and a gurney rolled and rattled its way across the porch.

Maybe she would follow Burt Johnston to the hospital in Winchester. Burt owned and operated the two veterinary clinics in the county. He'd taken care of her beloved collie, Maisey, twenty years ago. Couldn't hurt to ask him for a few details.

He'd tell his coffee-drinking buddies at breakfast in the morning anyway. He might as well tell Audrey now. After all, the newspaper gave him a discount on all his advertising. It was the least he could do.

A murder—even in self-defense—was as scarce as hen's teeth in Franklin County. Especially if it involved a possible mob-connected stranger from out of town and a quiet Mennonite woman who'd lived here her whole life.

Had all the makings of a feature that could be picked up by the Associated Press. This might be Audrey's lucky night.

Chapter Two

Audrey tossed her keys onto the table that sat next to the door. Lifting one foot and then the other, she removed her ruined shoes. She paused for a moment, her toes curling against the cool wood floor. The house was completely dark save for the lamp on the table where her keys lay. It felt so strange coming home to an empty house. Even now, after six months of living in her childhood home as an adult, the hollowness at times startled her.

Her mother had always been so cheerful and vibrant. No matter the season, the house had been filled with the scent and beauty of the flowers from her gardens. Even in the winter she had kept plants blooming in the Victorian-style greenhouse she had built when Audrey was a child. Every single year until the one before last, Mary Jo Anderson had won awards for her lovely gardens. Her gardening had always been her escape, her own special brand of chicken soup for the soul.

Reading had been Audrey's. She imagined it

was all those suspense novels that had made her
so bold as a reporter. She often told friends she
had lived a thousand lives through the books she
read. Growing up in a small town, books were
her escape.

She picked up her high heels and headed for
the staircase. The entire house remained stuck in
the Victorian era with few concessions to mod-
ern times: a more comfortable sofa in the den
and updated appliances in the kitchen. The paint
and wallpaper, though well maintained, boasted
the same pinks and burgundies from more than a
hundred and twenty years ago when the house was
built. Her great-great-grandmother who'd actually
commissioned the house had insisted on keeping
things exactly the way she'd wanted them. Mary
Jo, though not exactly a pink-and-burgundy lady,
had respectfully left the decorating scheme as the
late great Annette Anderson had decreed. Audrey's grandmother and great-grandmother had
done the same.

At the top of the stairs, Audrey glanced toward
the south end of the second-floor hall. The suite at
that end had belonged to her parents. How many
nights had she crept quietly through the darkness from her bedroom at the other end to those
towering double doors? Her father had always
scooped her up and nestled her between him and
her mother. A perk of being an only child.

Even after all these years, her heart squeezed at the memory of her father. She imagined that she would always miss him, no matter that he'd been gone for twenty-four years. Weary now, she made her way to her room, the same one she'd slept in growing up, and padded straight to the walk-in closet to put her damaged shoes away. She should probably just throw them out, but the little shoe repair shop on the corner of the square depended on folks like her to stay in business. No one understood the need for supporting local businesses better than Audrey. Though she was far from destitute, the expenses related to her mother's care and turning the newspaper around were quickly draining her savings.

She sighed as she hung up her jacket. Though her mother had changed hardly a thing around the house, Audrey had altered a couple of things right away. The first being to expand her closet into a decent-sized one. And still she'd had to downsize her wardrobe. Living in the limelight of investigative journalism for all those years had required an extensive wardrobe. Plus, she was reasonably sure she had a slight obsession with clothes, shoes in particular. With her work, it hadn't actually been a problem.

But that life was over.

Audrey closed the door of the closet as well as the one to the past.

No looking back. This was her life now, and it wasn't such a bad one.

She tossed her clutch purse onto a chair and reached for the zipper of her skirt. After leaving the Sauder farm she'd followed Burt to the hospital but had learned nothing. As she left the hospital and headed home, she dictated the story to Brian, her longtime friend and the editor at the *Winchester Gazette*, via her cell. Once she'd sent him the photos she'd snapped, he had laid out the story for tomorrow's front page. It would be tight, but since they were one of the few remaining small-town newspapers that still did their own printing, the job would get done. Newspapers landing on doorsteps and in stands tomorrow morning would showcase what little was known about the shooting. The article was already online.

Sarah Sauder was two or three years younger than Audrey. She remembered seeing her at the family-run bakery as a child and then as the woman behind the cash register since moving back to Winchester. Audrey popped in at least once every week. The Yoder Bakery, though located outside Winchester proper, was considered a local landmark. The peanut butter balls were to die for and her mother loved them. Audrey liked having a special treat for her mother when she visited. She also adored their blueberry scones. She bought those for herself, which was all the more reason not to drop by too often.

But the man who'd taken his last breath on Sarah Sauder's kitchen floor hadn't come to Buncombe Road for peanut butter balls or blueberry scones. And he sure hadn't broken into the century-old farmhouse looking for valuables to snatch. Branch Holloway's presence ruled out any possibility of the man's death being something less than serious trouble.

Wouldn't be drugs or human trafficking. Certainly not gunrunning. At least not involving the Sauders. The man had obviously connected the wrong identity with the house. But that still left the possibility that someone in Franklin County was up to no good and the trouble rippled all the way to the Windy City.

The skirt she'd worn tonight slid down her hips, then she stepped out of it. Frankly, she couldn't think of any criminal activities that rose to that level in which any of the locals, much less the Yoders—in this case the Sauders by marriage—would be involved. Of all people, Audrey was well aware of the reality that what one saw was rarely exactly what lay beneath the skin of others. But these were Mennonites.

She frowned as her fingers hesitated on the buttons of her blouse. She'd forgotten to ask Brian how he'd heard about the shooting. She assumed it was from the police scanner. She would ask him tomorrow.

The buzz of her cell echoed in the room, the sound muffled deep inside the clutch she'd tossed aside. She didn't dare ignore it. There could be breaking news in the shooting…or an issue at the paper.

Since taking over the *Winchester Gazette*, she'd realized how running the family business could consume one's life. As a crime reporter she had given herself completely to the story, but when the story was over there was typically some time before another came her way. Running the *Gazette* was entirely different. It was always there, an endless cycle of need for more content. Another story, another something to fill the pages—advertising. The newspaper had been in the Anderson family for nearly two centuries. How could she be the one to walk away? Her father would have wanted her to take over when his brother, Audrey's uncle Phillip, decided to retire.

She shivered. It wasn't like she'd had a choice. That decision had been taken from her years ago.

She dragged her cell from the clutch. When she had learned the developer who wanted to buy the *Gazette* planned to tear it down, she'd had to take control. The shiver turned into a chill that scurried deep into her bones.

The historic building could not be torn down. Ever.

At least not as long as Audrey was still breathing.

The caller ID read Pine Haven. A new kind of dread spread through Audrey's body. Pine Haven was her mother's residential care facility.

"Audrey Anderson." She held her breath. It had been two days since she'd visited her mom. What kind of daughter allowed forty-eight hours to pass without dropping by or at least calling?

"Ms. Anderson, this is Roberta Thompson at Pine Haven."

The worry in the other woman's voice sent another spear of uncertainty knifing through Audrey.

"Your mother is very agitated tonight. We need to sedate her but she insists on seeing you first. I know it's late but—"

"I'll be right there."

THE DRIVE TO Pine Haven on the other side of town took scarcely fifteen minutes and still it felt like forever. Audrey's heart pounded twice for every second that passed before she was parked and at the front entrance. The night guard waved her through. Evidently her mother had the facility's night shift all out of sorts.

Nurse Roberta Thompson waited for Audrey at the entrance to the Memory Care Unit. Roberta smiled sadly. "I'm so sorry I had to bother you at this hour, but she won't stay in her bed and she's demanding to see you. When a patient is this agitated we nearly always have to use sedation, but your mother's file says you prefer to be called first."

"Absolutely." Audrey held up her hands. "Please. You know I always want you to call. No matter the hour."

Roberta nodded. "Talk to her. You're what she needs right now. Then we'll get her settled for the night."

Mary Jo Anderson was pacing her room when Audrey walked through the door. Her short white hair was mussed, her long flannel gown rumpled as if she'd already tossed and turned all night.

"Mom."

Mary Jo's gaze settled on Audrey's. For a moment she stared, the haze of confusion and distance dulling her blue eyes. She was far away from this place, perhaps not in miles but in time. Audrey knew the look too well. When she came back home to buy the paper and to stay until she sorted out her future, Audrey had been startled by the episodes of total memory loss her mother suffered. Startled and heartbroken. How could she have deteriorated so without Audrey knowing it?

"Audrey." The haze cleared and her mother smiled.

Audrey closed the door and walked over to hug her. "What's going on? Nurse Thompson told me you're upset."

When Audrey drew back, her mother's smile was gone. "They'll find him and then you know what will happen."

The too-familiar apprehension stole back into Audrey's gut. "Let's sit down, Mom, okay? I'm really tired. I'm sure you must be, too."

She ushered her mom to the bed and they sat on the edge.

Mary Jo took in Audrey's jeans and sweater before settling her gaze on her face once more. "You're the prettiest girl I've ever seen in plain old blue jeans, Audrey Rose."

Audrey couldn't help smiling. "You always say that, Mom."

"It's true." Mary Jo sighed, turned away to stare at the wall on the other side of the room as if someone else had spoken to her. "I'm sorry I caused you all this trouble, sweetheart. You should be back in Washington. I've messed up everything."

Audrey put her arms around her mother's shoulders. "You didn't mess up a thing. Remember? I moved back to Winchester six months ago to buy the paper." The surprise in her mother's eyes warned that she'd forgotten. "I took over the *Gazette* for Uncle Phil. He wanted to retire."

She looked away, a classic indication she did not recall. The lines on her face appeared deeper than ever. *Worry*. Even with her memories fading, she still worried. Was that the curse of being a woman? A mother?

Or was it the secret they had been keeping for so long?

Audrey pushed away the thought. That was taken care of for now. No need for either of them to worry.

"We can't hide our secret forever," her mother whispered.

Mary Jo's words brought Audrey's attention back to her. She glanced at the door—couldn't help herself. No one needed to hear this. No doubt anyone who did overhear would think it was just the disease talking. Still, Audrey would feel better if her mother didn't mention that part of their past. "Mom, you don't need to worry about the secret. No one will ever know. I promise."

Her gaze latched onto Audrey's once more, the urgency there painful to look at. "You can't stop it. Fate or whatever they call it…the Lord. The Bible says so." She heaved a big breath. "They will find us out and it's my fault. All my fault."

She muttered those last three words over and over.

Audrey would need to check with Roberta to see if Mary Jo had any visitors today. Usually something set off this kind of episode. Maybe she'd somehow heard the news about the shooting on Buncombe Road. Audrey didn't see how that was possible. Could have been some other shooting or death. Sometimes startling events sent her mother off on a tangent. On those occasions, Audrey did all she could to soothe her frayed nerves and to guide her toward more comforting memories.

"Mom, do you remember my junior play? You had to make my costume. I was the nurse and you were so upset that I wasn't cast as Juliet."

"The costume was hideous." She shook her head. "You should have been Juliet."

Audrey laughed. "Well, Mrs. Bishop was the director and I guess she wanted her daughter to play the lead role."

Mary Jo chuckled. "I think the only thing worse than that costume was your dress for the senior prom."

"Oh." Audrey shuddered at the thought. The dress was one memory she had worked hard to exile. "It was absolutely awful."

Her mother rambled on about the dress order and the numerous fittings and how the garment still would not fit properly. Audrey had been reduced to tears at least twice until she'd decided enough was enough and had worn her favorite jeans and tee to the damned prom. Half the senior class as well as the school staff had been mortified; the other half couldn't have cared less. Audrey would wager that she was the only girl who had ever dared wear jeans to a prom in Franklin County, maybe in the whole state of Tennessee.

Colt had grinned and told her she was the most beautiful girl in the gymnasium—and maybe the world. The old ache that accompanied memories of her senior year squeezed deep inside Audrey's chest. She had been madly in love with Colt Tanner. They had been planning their future together since eighth grade when he sneaked a kiss on the school bus. That kiss had startled them both. The perfect balance of sweetness and innocence.

She had known the boy and then the man inside out. At least, she'd thought she had. But you never really know a person. Not really. When he'd married someone else—a pregnant-with-his-child someone else—Audrey had realized she could never trust anyone with her heart ever again. If Colt would break it, there was no hope with anyone else.

True to her decision, she never had. In December she would turn thirty-seven. Forty was right down the road. In all probability she would never know how it felt to hold her own child in her arms or to share her life with a man she loved the way her mother had loved her father. Of course her career had been immensely fulfilling—until things had gone so very wrong.

The newspaper would just have to be her baby, she supposed. Certainly the staff was like family. And she still had her mother. Well, most of the time, anyway.

Rather than wallowing in self-pity, Audrey listened as her mother talked on and on about the distant past—the good days, she called them. The ones before that awful year of darkness that came after her father's heart attack…and the secret that she and her mother would take to their graves.

Some things had to stay buried. There was no other option—not then and not now.

"Then you went off to become the celebrated investigative journalist," Mary Jo said after a long pause, her eyes gleaming with pride. "Your father would have been so proud. He never wanted you stuck here running that damned newspaper. He wanted you to explore the world, to conquer all the glass ceilings."

Except there really was no choice now. Six months ago her mother had called with the news that Phillip was retiring and a developer wanted to buy the paper. Said developer planned to demolish the old building and start fresh—his words. That could not happen. Not in this lifetime. The building had to stay exactly where it was for the foreseeable future.

"To tell you the truth, Mom, I was tired of all the travel and the limelight." Audrey waved off the career that had once been her singular focus. "Let someone else have a turn at being the best." She winked at her mother. "I couldn't hog all the glamour forever."

Mary Jo smiled and patted Audrey on the leg. "You were always such a thoughtful girl. I'll never forget the time you came home and bagged up all your clothes to take to that little girl whose house had burned down. I finally convinced you that we could take her shopping for new clothes. You really made your father and I proud. I know he has watched your career from heaven."

There was another secret Audrey planned to keep. Her mother would never know—nor would anyone else for that matter—that her career had gone to hell in a handbasket. She'd made a mistake. Ten years at the top of her game and she'd made a totally dumb, foolish mistake. She'd wanted the story so badly, she'd trusted a source without going through all the usual steps to verify that source. She had allowed her friendship with that source to guide her, and she'd rushed to beat everyone else. She'd screwed up.

Big-time.

Bottom line, she had no one to blame but herself. While she had been licking her wounds, her mother had called with news about Phil's retirement. Audrey had done what she had to do. She'd zoomed home and bought out her uncle's portion of the family business. With her savings basically depleted after that, she'd decided to stay on and try turning the paper around. No one knew how to lay out a titillating story better than Audrey. She could have the paper thriving again within a year. No problem. An entire human could be made in less time. Of course she could do it. It was the perfect distraction. If she was busy saving the family legacy, she didn't have to think about the rubble that was once her career.

Or the secret that no one else could ever know.

Her mother laid her head on Audrey's shoulder, exhaustion overtaking her now that the manic episode had passed.

But it was coming home to do what must be done that served up another cold hard reality to Audrey. Her mother was not well. The forgetfulness and absentmindedness were not merely age or the overabundance of civic commitments to which she had obligated herself for the past thirty-five years.

Mary Jo Anderson had dementia. If Audrey had come home more often, she would have realized the lost keys and missed appointments her mother had laughed about on the phone were more than forgetfulness. Far more. But she had been too busy with her illustrious career. She had called her mother every week, sometimes twice, but she hadn't gotten home nearly as often as she should have.

But she was here now. And as her father always said, "when life gives you lemons, you make lemonade."

Tonight's shooting was a perfect example. Nothing promised a bump in circulation like a potential homicide.

Chapter Three

Colt leaned against the cab of his truck and blew out a weary breath. Burt had taken the body. Rather than deliver the outsider to a local funeral home, he was headed to the state medical examiner's office to turn over the body for an autopsy. The department's two-man crime scene unit had gone over the Sauder home with a fine-tooth comb.

The biggest thing missing at the moment was Sarah Sauder's husband. He was supposed to be headed home from a funeral he'd attended up in Hendersonville, but he still hadn't made it back. Seemed to Colt that the man would have moved heaven and earth to get to his wife and children after hearing about the shooting. Sarah and the kids had apparently given up hope of his arrival, since they'd left and gone to her father's house. The lights in the Sauder home were out now and the doors were locked up tight. Colt had suggested Sarah and her kids stay with family until they released the scene. There would need to be another look tomorrow for potential evidence. Not that Colt really expected to find any.

The evening had been a tough one for Sarah. To have strangers walking through her home and touching her belongings was not something to which folks in the Mennonite community were accustomed. They were private people. Kept to themselves and stayed out of trouble. This was not the norm by any means.

US Marshal Branch Holloway paced the road just far enough from Colt's truck to ensure he didn't overhear his cell phone conversation. Branch had an outstanding reputation with the Marshals Service as far as Colt knew, but something had landed him in Franklin County assigned to the federal courthouse last year. Whatever it was, it couldn't have been good. Winchester wasn't exactly a hotbed of criminal activity, and there damned sure wasn't much of anything that rose to the federal level in Franklin County.

Tonight, apparently, was an exception.

Branch had said the victim was some button man for the Chicago mob. Beyond that he'd been pretty tight-lipped. Didn't sit well with Colt. This was his county and by God he needed to know the full details of what had transpired in the Sauder home tonight. He had no intention of relinquishing control over this investigation until he had no other choice. The safety of the residents in this county was his responsibility, not Branch Holloway's.

Branch tucked his phone away and headed toward Colt. Colt pushed away from the truck and set his hands on his hips. "So what did your former boss have to say?"

"I was right. The victim is Tony Marcello." Branch glanced toward the darkened house. "This was no random break-in, Colt. Marcello is the kind of guy who does the dirty work. Collects on loans. Acts as an enforcer or bodyguard. Bottom line, he does whatever he's ordered to do. I can't see a guy like that making this kind of mistake."

Oh hell. "So you're saying the Sauders are involved in some sort of mob business." Colt couldn't see it. Not in a million years.

"Sure looks that way." Branch matched Colt's stance, hands on hips, boots wide apart, as if they were about to see who was the fastest draw. "I've only been back a year so I'm not up to speed on everyone in the area. How well do you know Wesley Sauder?"

"How well do you know any of the Mennonite folks?" Colt tossed back at him. Branch grew up in Winchester. He knew the deal. "They keep to themselves. Yet they're good neighbors, good citizens. Never any trouble—at least if there is any, they take care of it amid their own ranks." He shook his head. "I can't see what you're suggesting by any stretch of the imagination."

"But," Branch said, shrugging, "Wesley was an outsider until what? Ten years ago?"

That much was true. "He moved here about ten years ago, yeah." Colt considered the answers the man's wife had given to the interview questions. "Sarah said he came from Markham, Illinois."

"Markham's not so far from Chicago."

Colt heaved another sigh. "We'll know more when we've run Sauder's prints."

Colt had instructed one of his forensic techs to lift prints from the wooden arms of the rocking chair next to the fireplace. Sarah had glanced at the empty chair when she spoke of her husband. Colt figured the rocker was the chair her husband used.

"There's no Wesley Sauder from Illinois or Tennessee in the database," Branch said. "So if the husband is who he says he is, you won't find anything there."

"Then again, if we get a hit from a database then we'll know he isn't who he says he is." Damn. Branch's contact was able to access the needed information in an instant. Colt didn't have those kinds of resources. As much as he wanted to be grateful for the potential assist in this case, he was mostly ticked off. "Otherwise, the only thing we'll know for sure is that Sauder doesn't have a criminal record and he hasn't needed a background check that required his prints."

"Guess so." Branch was already marking his territory. He wanted this case.

"We could debate what this shooting boils down to all night and we still won't be any closer to the truth than we are right now." Colt wasn't relinquishing a damned thing until he understood exactly what they were dealing with. "We need to do this right, Branch. By the book. No getting ahead of ourselves."

Colt didn't know all the details of why Branch had left Chicago and ended up back in his hometown on a babysitting assignment, but there would be plenty to the story and little if any of it résumé-worthy.

"We'll play it your way for now." Branch glanced once more at the Sauder home. "I'll touch base with you tomorrow."

Colt gave him a nod of agreement and watched him get into his truck and drive away. He sure as hell wished Melvin Yoder wasn't on his deathbed. Tomorrow Colt would check in with the family to see if a short visit with the patriarch of the Mennonite community in Franklin County might be possible. Yoder would know his son-in-law better than anyone. Sauder would never have been able to marry Yoder's daughter if he hadn't approved of the man.

Colt's father and Yoder had been good friends. At least as close as an outsider could be with a member of the closed community. Hopefully that friendship would help now. If the older man's health would tolerate a visit, Colt needed some insight into Wesley Sauder. What the hell kind of man would be a no-show when his family needed him?

There was only one plausible answer: a man who had something to hide.

Colt loaded into his truck, took one last look at the farmhouse. Whatever Sarah Sauder and her husband were hiding, he would find it.

COLT HADN'T MUCH more than pulled into the driveway at his house when another problem cropped up. His son, Key, pulled in right behind him, and it was well beyond his curfew on a school night.

Colt sat stone-still behind the wheel of his truck. He'd already shut off the engine, and the headlights had faded to darkness. His son had no idea he was out here. Probably thought his overbearing, out-of-touch-with-reality daddy was in bed asleep by now. As Colt watched, the eighteen-year-old climbed out of his truck and closed the door quietly. He glanced around the yard and started toward the house.

Staggered toward the house.

Colt swore under his breath. He watched his

only child beat a crooked path to his bedroom window, which he subsequently opened and struggled clumsily through, ultimately falling into the house. If Colt was lucky, right on his head. Maybe it would knock some sense into him. The boy was hell-bent on trouble. He'd had everything he ever wanted handed to him on a silver platter—including that brand-new pickup his Granddaddy Wilhelm gave him. The real problem was that between his momma and his granddaddy, the kid was spoiled rotten. Colt was the only one who issued any sort of rules, and shared custody ensured that at least half the time his son had no rules whatsoever.

He was headed down a bad path.

But this was the first time Colt had known him to come home drunk. He glanced in the rearview mirror at the shiny red truck parked behind him. The boy had been driving while intoxicated. Colt had witnessed it with his own eyes. All the other dumb stuff he overlooked was nothing to compare with this. Driving under the influence was not something he could pretend not to notice in order to keep the peace.

"Damn it all to hell."

Colt emerged from his truck, slammed the door and headed for the house he'd inherited from his daddy—the one thing Colt hadn't lost in the divorce. By the time he reached Key's bedroom, his son was lying on the floor where he'd fallen and was snoring up a storm. Shaking his head, Colt closed and locked the window. He picked up the fob to the boy's truck and tucked it into his pocket. No more driving for at least a month. Waking up his son and giving him what for at the moment would be a pointless waste of energy. Arguing with a drunk got both parties nowhere fast.

Morning would be soon enough to tackle this unpleasant task. He considered helping his son into the bed but decided he should sleep it off right where he'd fallen. His cell phone had tumbled from his pocket and lay next to him. Colt made another decision. The kid didn't need his phone for a while, either. A set of wheels and a cell phone were luxuries that not all kids his son's age enjoyed. Why should Key have access to those and more when he couldn't obey the rules?

Disgusted and exhausted, Colt wandered to his bedroom. He placed his hat on the bureau. He needed a shower and a beer. He thought of his son passed out on the floor in the other bedroom. Maybe he'd forgo the beer. He dropped onto the side of the bed and pulled off first one boot and then the other, tossing the well-worn footwear to the floor. Socks went next. He'd worn cowboy boots his whole life. His daddy bought him his first pair as soon as he could walk. If his dad were still here he would know what to do to steer Key in the right direction.

Sometimes Colt wondered if his ex-wife allowed the boy to run wild just to get back at Colt for the divorce. God knew Colt had never been allowed to behave this way, and he damned sure hadn't intended for his son to end up on this plunge into stupidity. But Karen let the boy do anything he wanted. She'd named him after her daddy, Keyton. Colt had been good with that, since his son would carry the Tanner surname. He'd wanted to be fair. But Karen Wilhelm had never played fair in her life. Key hadn't been a year old the first time Colt caught her cheating. He'd put up with her lies for ten years in an attempt to hold his family together. Then he'd had enough.

He peeled off his shirt and reached for his belt. Key's cell phone blasting a rap tune stopped him. *Mom* appeared on the screen. Colt tapped the screen and answered with the same "yo" his son always used.

"Baby, I just wanted to make sure you got home all right. You were a little drunk."

Outrage coursed through Colt's veins. "You allowed our son to drive when he'd been drinking?"

Silence screamed across the line.

"Why do you have Key's phone?"

The cold fury in her voice was nothing compared to the white-hot rage gushing through Colt at the moment. "Because he dropped it while he was climbing through his bedroom window. At the moment he's passed out on the floor."

"I'm… I'm sure he wasn't drinking that much when he left here. He must have stopped at a friend's on the way home."

Liar.

"He won't be driving for a good long while. And he won't be available by cell, either."

"My father gave him that truck. You don't have any right to take it."

"You would rather I arrest him for driving under the influence? I can definitely do that, and I don't need your or your daddy's permission to do it."

"You wouldn't dare."

He laughed. "I arrested you, didn't I?"

Of course, her rich daddy had hired the best lawyer in the county to take care of the situation. So far, he'd managed that feat five times. No wonder their son felt no fear of consequences. He'd watched his mother skate out of trouble his whole life. Including ten years of Colt looking the other way while she screwed her way through the county's male population.

"My father will be calling you in the morning."

The call ended.

Colt turned the phone off and shoved it into the

pillowcase of the pillow he didn't use. His boy would never think to look there. God knew his momma wasn't coming anywhere near Colt's bed.

He shucked his jeans and boxers and headed for the shower. While he waited for the water to warm he thought of the biggest mistake of his life.

Hurting Rey.

Each time he saw her he was reminded of the enormous mistake he'd made. How the hell had he let her get away? He almost laughed at the idea. He hadn't *let* her do anything. Audrey Rose Anderson did what she damned well pleased, then and now.

She had been his everything since he was a kid. If he was honest with himself, he had been fascinated with her since the first day of kindergarten when she kicked the boy who laughed at him for crying. Cutting the other kid some slack, he had no idea Colt's mother had been dying with cancer. No matter that she'd been so sick, she'd wanted to take her little boy to his first day of school. When she'd left him in the classroom the tears had streamed down his face. Colt had been terrified she would die before he was back at home with her.

After kicking the laughing kid in the shin, Audrey had walked up to Colt and said, "I like your boots. You want to sit at my table?"

They had been friends from that day on. And

then he'd fallen in love with her. Head over heels in love. Even now, thinking of her made it hard to breathe.

"You screwed that up, dumbass."

Colt stepped into the shower and drowned the memories beneath the spray of hot water.

There were some transgressions for which there was no forgiveness. Rey reminded him every chance she got.

Chapter Four

"Adding the plea for information was genius." Audrey laid this morning's edition of the *Gazette* on her desk. "Good call, Brian."

Brian Peterson grinned. "I learned from the best."

His enthusiasm was contagious and Audrey felt her own lips pull into a smile, no matter that she was utterly exhausted this morning. As her mom would say, "as tired when she got up as she had been when she went to bed." "My uncle was a good mentor."

"I meant *you*," Brian clarified.

Audrey laughed. "You were helping my uncle run this paper long before I came back to take over."

"I watched your career," Brian argued. "Learned a lot from your approach to a story."

"Flattery will get you everywhere," she pointed out.

"I know." He lifted an eyebrow at her. "I survived kindergarten through senior year with you as one of my best friends. I think I know you pretty well."

"It's a miracle either one of us survived."

Brian was a good friend, had been since they were kids in school. She would never forget freshman year sitting at his side, just the two of them, at a table in the school cafeteria the day another former friend announced to the world that Brian was gay. One of her best memories of that entire year happened on that day. Colt, big football star, had swaggered over to their table and sat down on the other side of Brian. Her chest filled with remembered pride. What had happened to the guy who stood by his friends through thick and thin to make him break the heart of the girl madly in love with him?

"You're thinking about Colt."

Brian's words snapped her back to the here and now. She blinked, rearranged her expression into a frown. "What?"

But her faux look of surprise didn't fool her old friend for a moment. "Uh-huh. That's what I thought."

Rather than have that conversation, she moved on. "Have any calls with useful information come in this morning?"

"A few," he said, "but don't try changing the subject. How long can you hold an eighteen-year-old's drunken mistake against him?"

Okay, so he wasn't going to let it go. Winning the football championship senior year had culminated in a party at a cabin belonging to the family of one of the players. Everyone had gone. Except Audrey. She'd had the flu. The following spring the whole school knew the rest of the story—Karen Wilhelm was obviously pregnant. Karen was only too happy to name Colt as the father. Audrey barely managed to finish out the school year and stumble through graduation. If not for Brian and Sasha, her two best friends, she would have skipped the ceremonial stuff altogether.

"Forever," she said in answer to Brian's question—the one he asked about once a month. "Have any of the calls offered leads we might want to follow up on?" she asked again.

He sighed and shook his head. "Not yet."

"We need to know more about this Wesley Sauder." Audrey walked over to the large chalkboard her father had used. It took up the better part of one wall. Her father had kept all sorts of notes on it, but he'd always kept one small corner free for her to draw and doodle whenever she visited his office. By the time she was in sixth grade she generally walked to the paper rather than go home. She'd done her homework right here in this office.

"You have basically everything we know outlined." Brian joined her at the chalkboard. "Sauder moved here ten years ago from Illinois. The way I heard the story, he came upon Melvin Yoder in a pasture being charged by a bull or something like that. Saved his life. Yoder took him under his wing in the community, and the guy married the older man's daughter. Ten years and four kids later, he's way up the hierarchy in the Mennonite community. Mr. Yoder is very ill, and rumor has it, everyone is looking to Sauder to hold things together moving forward."

Audrey scanned the notes they'd taped to the board. "Sauder is forty-eight, more than a decade older than his wife."

Brian tapped a photo of Sarah he'd dug up from an article done on the Yoder Bakery a couple of years ago. "She is the only daughter Yoder claims and his middle child. At twenty-four and unmarried when the accident happened, she was bordering on old maid status. Giving his daughter as a wife to the man who saved his life killed two birds with one stone, so to speak."

"Seriously?" Audrey couldn't believe anyone still considered an unmarried woman in her midtwenties an old maid.

Brian held up his hands. "Their views are less progressive. We all know you're not an old maid just because you're single and thirtysomething."

Choosing to ignore the subject, she said, "You

said the only daughter he claims. Does he have another one? I don't remember another one."

"Bethany. She's several years younger than us. She's thirty-one, maybe. She dropped out of school at sixteen and disappeared. Ran off to Nashville to be a singer."

"What happened to her after that?" Maybe that was why Audrey didn't remember her.

"Fame and riches weren't in the cards for her, I guess. Eventually she came back, but her family shunned her or maybe she shunned them. She works as a waitress at one of the bars on the other side of town. Never married. Just lives her life."

Like you, Audrey.

She thought of the birth announcement she'd noticed in today's paper. Another of her high school classmates was having a child. She and Sasha Lenoir were the only ones left who hadn't married. Even Brian had a husband. Last year they had adopted a little girl. Audrey had shoes. Lots of shoes. And a huge house that felt so very empty. At least Sasha still had her career. She was the best crisis manager in the Northeast. It had been far too long since she and Audrey had spent time together. They needed a girls' weekend. Time to catch up and relax. Time to just be.

"Back in elementary school there was a girl from the class above us who spent a lot of time with Sarah," Brian said.

Audrey dismissed the notions of getaways and looked at Brian in surprise. "Really? Someone from our school?" The Mennonite community had their own school. They didn't socialize with outsiders beyond what was necessary to conduct business.

"Remember the old Yarborough place?"

"The abandoned house that used to be a rental?" The Yarboroughs were long dead when Audrey was a child. Whoever had inherited the place lived in another state but opted to keep the home. One of the local real estate companies had maintained and rented the house until a few years ago. The property was right next to the Yoder place.

Brian nodded, a glint in his eye. "Nikki owns the diner now. She lived in the old Yarborough house all during elementary school. I wouldn't be surprised if she and Sarah have remained friends."

"Nikki Wells?" Audrey vaguely remembered the older girl.

"She's Nikki Slater now. Two kids." Brian sent her a pointed look. "I say this not to remind you that everyone we know is having babies, but because she will show off the pictures, so you might as well be prepared."

"Thanks. I'll head that way. I could use a decent cup of coffee." Audrey smiled as she rounded her desk and reached for her purse. She loved her old friend, but the man did not know the first thing about making coffee.

Brian crossed his arms over his chest. "I make a perfect cup of coffee. Unless you're one of those people who prefer coffee capable of being substituted for asphalt patch."

She flashed him a patient smile. "See you later." Audrey headed for the door.

"One more thing," he called behind her.

She paused at the door. Brian really was her best friend in the world. She adored him despite his inability to understand the purpose of coffee. She needed it strong enough to make her pay attention and packed with enough caffeine to keep her that way. "Yes?"

"Braden House wants to know if you're interested in spearheading another fund-raiser this year. They're still praising you for surpassing their goal last year. No one has ever raised as much money as you did."

Braden House was a refuge for abused women. "I would love to spearhead this year's fund-raiser. It's not until October, right?"

He nodded. "I knew you would. That's why I told them yes yesterday."

Audrey gave him a thumbs-up. "Thanks."

"You are such a do-gooder, Anderson." He rolled his eyes. "You need to funnel some of that energy toward a personal life."

"I am extremely happy with my personal life just as it is—*personal*."

She managed to get the door open this time before he interrupted. "We really need to have someone find out where that water in the basement is coming from," he called after her. "I checked last night and there's a little more than last time. It's not that much water, but it worries me that it's more than just dampness seeping up from the concrete. It's actual water standing on the floor."

Even as her heart pounded harder, Audrey held up a hand and produced a decisive tone. "I'll take care of it. Don't worry. This building is more than two hundred years old. There's probably an underground spring or something. We just need to get all that concrete resealed with that whatever-it's-called stuff that stops water penetration."

"You're the boss."

Audrey laughed at the comment before walking out of her office. In many ways Brian was far more the boss than she was. She didn't mind sharing that title with him. She descended the stairs and walked directly to the rear exit, grateful the lobby was empty and the receptionist was tied up on the phone. By the time she reached the small employee parking lot just out the back door, her heart rate had settled to some semblance of normal. She would call someone about the basement. There was no denying the issue any longer. Just not today.

She drew in a deep, calming breath of the cool morning air. She was grateful for the matching sweater she'd chosen to go along with her plum-colored trousers. The high temperature would reach into the sixties by noon, but this morning it was well below that mark.

Settling into the driver's seat, she fisted her fingers to rid them of the lingering trembles. For a moment she stared at the building that had been in her family for more than two centuries. She rarely came in through the front lobby. The offices were set up the old-fashioned way, in a ring around the second floor overlooking the expansive lobby. There was a large and a small conference room. Downstairs, the lobby was filled with *Gazette* history. Third graders from the elementary schools toured the exhibit every year. Beyond the lobby, the supply room, the break room and the massive space where the papers were printed consumed the rest of the square footage. The basement had never been used for anything other than storage of unused equipment or ancient files. The maintenance parts of the building, like the heating and cooling systems, were housed there as well.

No reason to be overly concerned about a little water in a basement. It had happened numerous times before.

Not a priority for now.

THE CORNER DINER was on the southeast corner of the square. It was a lunch staple of the downtown square and courthouse crowd. Nikki Wells Slater's family started the diner in the 1940s. At eight forty-five in the morning the breakfast crowd had dwindled.

Audrey sat down at one end of the deserted bar and ordered coffee. Several other business owners smiled as they passed on their way out or paused to say good morning. Audrey sipped her coffee while Nikki took an order at a table. Once she'd delivered it to the order station and turned back to the bar, Audrey smiled.

Nikki wandered over. "You ready for a refill?"

Audrey shook her head. "I'm good. How are you, Nikki?" She had grabbed a quick lunch in the diner on several occasions, but she and Nikki hadn't actually talked beyond a hello or thank you.

"I'm great." She smiled and gestured to the wall next to the order window where photos of her two children, a girl and a boy, formed a cheerful collage. "My kids are happy and healthy and so far my husband is still trying to impress me."

Audrey laughed. "You can't ask for more than that."

"That's the truth." Nikki considered her a moment. "So, how are you, Rey?"

"I'm settling in. Circulation is up in print and in online subscriptions. I'm happy."

The other woman's expression shifted to a more serious one. "How's your momma?"

Audrey shrugged. "Some days are better than others, but all in all she's okay. Thank you for asking."

Nikki grabbed a towel and wiped the counter next to Audrey. "That's good. She used to come in here all the time for my momma's lemon pie. She said it was the best pie in the world."

"I've taken it to her a few times since I've been back." One of these days Audrey might even try a slice herself. "How are your parents?"

Nikki's parents had retired and moved to Florida last year. Even though Winchester was a small town, a lot had changed since Audrey left for college. Thank goodness for Brian. He had spent days when Audrey first moved back to Winchester bringing her up to speed on who had died or moved or married, and anything else he considered relevant. People around here expected you to ask about their kin. Weddings, baby showers and funerals were necessary social events. Miss one and your name was tarnished.

"They miss their grandbabies but they love life on the beach. We go down four or five times a year and spend a week. They come here a couple times a year so it's not so bad. They're happy, that's what matters."

"Are you still friends with Sarah Yoder?"

Nikki studied Audrey for a moment. "She's Sarah Sauder now, but then I'm sure you know that already."

Audrey nodded. "I do. I was at her house last night but I didn't have the opportunity to speak with her. I was hoping you could help me set the story straight for Sarah. No one hates inaccurate news more than me."

Wariness slipped into the other woman's eyes. "How do you mean set the story straight?"

"You know, when things like this happen, there are always folks who want to make the real victim the bad guy. Sarah and I were never friends, but my father and her father were. My father thought very highly of Melvin Yoder. I'm certain he didn't raise a murderer. Sarah did what she had to do to protect her children and herself. I want people to know that before the rumors and gossip muddy the waters."

Audrey said this with as much righteous indignation as she could muster. And every word was true. Capturing the right story was immensely important to her.

"Of course she did," Nikki muttered. "Anyone who says different is a fool and a liar. Sarah is the gentlest, sweetest person I know. She wouldn't hurt a fly, much less kill a man, unless there was no other choice."

Audrey leaned forward. "That's exactly what

I said. But you know those hotline calls come in, and since they're anonymous, people think they can say the most hurtful and ridiculous things." This, too, was true. Though it hadn't happened yet, it would. It always did. "We need to set the record straight."

"I'm sure Sarah told the police someone had been hanging around her place. A stranger sitting out by the road in his black car just watching day in and day out." Nikki's lips formed a grim line. "She said Wesley was out of town and she was nervous. I don't blame her for shooting him after he broke in."

"She probably told her brothers how he was watching her place." The missing brothers were another detail that didn't sit right with Audrey. Where were those three strapping Yoder men when their sister needed help? Not a single one had shown up last night. Something was wrong with that picture, too.

"She couldn't." Nikki leaned across the counter. "Jacob's wife was having a baby. Aaron was at home with their father. Mr. Yoder can't be left alone now. He's very sick and his wife passed away last year."

Audrey nodded her understanding. "What about Benjamin?"

"Benjamin and Sarah aren't on speaking terms." Nikki shook her head. "I guess he's still upset that

Wesley—Sarah's husband—sort of took the spot he'd expected to hold as the oldest son."

Good point. "I didn't think of that," Audrey admitted. "I'm sure Benjamin was disappointed at not stepping into his father's shoes."

"The decision created quite the divide. I can't say that I blame Benjamin, but Sarah loves her husband. She supports him over her brother. It's what God intended. Her daddy's decision was his decision, not hers."

"Speaking of brothers." Audrey smiled. "How's your brother? I hear the kids around town love him." Charlie Wells was the sweetest guy. He and Audrey had worked together on the school paper. Why couldn't she have fallen for him?

How come she asked herself that same question about every nice guy she had ever known?

Nikki grinned. "Charlie loves being a doctor. He's the first one in the family to even attend college. I can't believe he took it all the way." She laughed, her fondness for her brother clear in her voice. "Who would've thought that my goofy baby brother would end up a pediatrician?"

"Look at you," Audrey countered. "You're running this place all on your own. The renovations you did last year are amazing. You've done pretty well yourself, Nikki."

She blushed, ducked her head. "Thank you.

Coming from a big-city girl like you, that's a real compliment."

Audrey waved her off. "If I can take care of the *Gazette* as well as you have the diner, I'll be happy."

Nikki looked around as if confirming no one was paying attention to their private conversation. "You should talk to Aaron. You didn't hear this from me, but I hear there was some sort of disagreement between Mr. Yoder and Wesley a few months back. By then Mr. Yoder was already bedridden and he'd single-handedly convinced the whole community to look to Sauder for guidance. Whatever happened, the two men don't speak anymore. Sarah won't talk about it but I get the feeling it's related to something the old man believes about his son-in-law. Some part of his past that he learned from visiting family who came down from Illinois last year."

"Something from Sauder's past?"

Nikki shrugged. "I don't know for sure. Sarah wouldn't talk about it, but something changed between Mr. Yoder and Wesley. Her brothers are upset with him as well. With that rift going on, I doubt she shared her worries with any of them. Now this man shows up breaking into their home and Sarah shoots him. Whatever's going on, it's not right. I'm worried that Sarah's in trouble."

Audrey was ecstatic to learn all these details but why would Nikki spill her guts like this? They had never really been friends, only acquaintances. She'd expected to have to wrangle information from her. And if Nikki really was worried about her friend, why not tell the sheriff? This didn't feel right.

"I'm grateful you've shared your feelings," Audrey confessed. "But to tell the truth, I'm surprised you've been so forthcoming."

Nikki looked around again. "I know you've been gone a long time, Audrey. Maybe you've forgotten that in small towns people take sides. They form opinions based on what they think they know without ever looking at the facts. No offense to Sheriff Tanner and his deputies, but they're not going to look beyond the idea that a stranger showed up in town and broke into a home and ended up dead. End of story. They won't dig around beneath the surface. Why should they? But something's wrong and I think Sarah is scared. She won't even talk to me anymore. Brian told me that no one knows how to dig up the truth better than you. Help my friend, that's all I ask."

So this had been a setup. At least it was the kind Audrey appreciated. "I'll do all I can, you have my word."

"Keep my name out of it if at all possible," Nikki urged. "Sarah is my friend and I don't want to hurt her. I'm just worried and that's the only reason I'm telling you all this."

"Trust me," Audrey assured her. "I have never divulged an anonymous source." Even when she'd wanted to do so after a source let her down. She had taken the fall. Good reporters always did. A good source was priceless. Do them wrong and you lost them and your reputation. In her entire career she never betrayed one and she never lost one. She wasn't about to start now.

The bell over the entrance jingled and Nikki drew away and called, "Morning, Sheriff. Coffee?"

Audrey placed the cash on the counter for her coffee and slid off the stool. The diner was empty save for the cowboy who had just swaggered in. As she watched, Colt lowered onto a stool midway down the counter without so much as glancing her way. He placed his hat on the stool next to him and ran a hand through his black hair. So, this was his way of avoiding any questions she might have.

She never had been put off by anyone's *ignore* mode. With that in mind, she marched down to where Colt sat and leaned against the counter. "Well, good morning to you, too, Sheriff."

He gave her a nod. "Morning, Rey."

"Anything new on the investigation?"

His gaze glued to the menu on the wall—a menu he likely knew by heart already—he moved his head from side to side. "Nothing I can talk about, anyway."

He would have been better served if he'd kept his response to nothing more than the shake of his head. "I take it Branch confirmed the identity of the big guy with the red hair who died on Sarah Sauder's kitchen floor last night?"

He turned to her, his gray eyes narrowed. "Has Branch been talking to you?"

She smiled at the idea that she'd just hit a nerve. Colt had always been jealous of Branch. Then again, what male wouldn't be? Branch was a good-looking *single* man. He'd been a big-shot football star back in high school and college, and he was still a hometown hero. But then, so was Colt.

"Branch understands the value of having a resource in the media on his side." Not exactly a lie, merely an avoidance of the actual question.

"Anthony Marcello is trouble, Rey."

Nikki placed a steaming cup of black coffee in front of Colt. He nodded his thanks and she moved on. The Corner Diner was a popular spot for business lunches and small gatherings. Nikki had worked there since she was a little girl. She had learned when to linger and when to give her patrons the space they needed for private conversations. Still, Audrey imagined she knew more secrets than anyone in town except maybe the stylists in the local salons.

"Maybe so, but he can hardly create any problems now—he's dead." She smiled at the way the lines of frustration gathered around his eyes, and his lips flattened into a grim line. Lips she had kissed about a thousand times.

Do not go there, Audrey.

"The problem is—" Colt shifted on the stool, his knee bumping her thigh and sending a zing of electricity through her "—Marcello has friends. Dangerous friends. You don't need to go chasing down that rabbit hole, Rey. You need to stay out of this investigation or there will be trouble for you...for all of us."

Chicago. Dangerous. Oh yeah, the dead guy was connected to a crime syndicate. It was the only logical explanation.

"Hmm. I can see you're very concerned for my safety, Sheriff." She cocked her head and stared at him. "But you see, I have a job to do, too, and that's to keep the community informed. Remember? We had this discussion last night. I'm sure they'll want to know what in the world the mob would be doing around here."

Before he could toss a practiced answer back at her, she added, "You know how people talk. The rumors will be worse than the truth."

Chapter Five

Colt wanted to shake the woman. The problem was if he put his hands anywhere on her body he would have an even bigger problem than keeping the citizens of his county safe and calm. The last thing he needed was for anyone to panic.

Before he could muster a proper comeback, she said, "Have a nice day, Sheriff."

He turned on the stool and watched Audrey walk away. The gentle sway of her hips made him sigh. Why the hell couldn't they figure this thing out and stop playing games?

"Here you go, Sheriff."

Reluctantly he twisted around to find that Nikki had prepared his untouched coffee to go. He grabbed the cup and gave her a nod. "Thanks."

She smiled. "You better hurry or she's going to get away."

He didn't bother to mention that Rey had gotten away long ago. Instead, Colt settled his hat into place and headed out the door. Rey was already climbing into her car when he caught up with her. "Look, I didn't mean to be so short with you, Rey."

She stood in the vee created by the open car door. "I'm not sure what you mean, Sheriff." She slipped on her sunglasses and waited for him to explain.

Damn, she never made things easy. He planted his free hand on his hip to prevent inadvertently touching her. "I had a rough night and I guess I sort of took it out on you."

Her eyebrows went up in surprise. "Did you stay too late at that saloon over in Kelso? Or maybe you did your drinking at home." She tore off the dark eyewear, leaned over the car door and put her face closer to his. "Your eyes do look a little bloodshot."

Before he could stop himself, he leaned down, almost nose to nose. "I was at the crime scene until almost midnight and then I went home. The problem was my son came home about that same time. He was intoxicated. He could have gotten himself or someone else killed driving in that condition. So, yeah, alcohol was involved but I wasn't the one drinking it."

Her breath caught and she drew away. "I'm sorry to hear that." She slid the sleek black glasses back into place but not before he could read the concern in her eyes. "I'm certain you were very upset." Her fingers tightened on the car door. "I'm glad he made it home safely."

"Thanks." He straightened, tried to figure a way to carry on a reasonable conversation with her. But every damned time they said more than a half a dozen words to each other they ended up bickering. "I meant what I said, Rey. If Branch is right about this mob connection, we could be looking at some serious trouble. I don't want you getting yourself in the line of fire."

She smiled but it wasn't the friendly kind. "I know how to handle myself, Sheriff. You don't need to worry about me."

Before she could turn away, his right hand settled on hers, trapping it between the cool metal of the door and his palm. The feel of her skin made his gut clench with need. How many nights had he fought the covers dreaming of her? "I do worry. I worry about everyone I care about."

"I'll keep that in mind."

She tugged her hand free of his and dropped behind the wheel. He closed her door, watched her buckle up, back out of the parking slot and drive away.

Well, at least she hadn't told him to mind his own business. Progress, he supposed. The bell at the top of the courthouse tolled the hour. He might as well head back to the office for his meeting with Branch. The sooner they figured out what

Tony Marcello was doing in Winchester, the sooner he could protect the citizens of his county.

BRANCH WAS STUDYING the awards on the office walls as Colt walked through the door. "Sorry to keep you waiting."

Branch extended his hand. Colt gripped it, gave it a shake.

"Not a problem," the marshal assured him. "I was catching up on your career highlights." He jerked his head toward the photos and plaques. "You're doing a good job, Colt. I know your daddy would be proud."

"Thanks. You need coffee or something?"

Branch shook his head. "I'm good." He sat down in one of the two chairs in front of Colt's desk. His trademark Stetson sat in the other.

Colt had always been a Resistol man. He hung his hat on the rack and took a seat behind his desk. "You have any updated information on this Tony Marcello?"

"He was a button man for the Cicero crime family. The Ciceros have been operating illegal activities in Chicago for decades. Marcello has been loosely linked to their operations for the past fifteen or so years. From what we know, he takes care of cleanups mostly. My guess is the family sent him down here to handle some unfinished business."

Colt braced his forearms on his desk. "You think Wesley Sauder is the unfinished business." Damned sure looked that way from where Colt was sitting. He would be the first to say coincidences were hard to ignore when they involved murder.

"I do." Branch nodded. "We need to find Sauder before the next guy they send does. And you can take this to the bank—they will keep sending one of their hired guns until this is finished."

"We can do this together," Colt offered, and then qualified, "but this is my investigation."

Branch held up his hands. "I'm here to assist you in any way you need. I'm happy to leave the investigation in your capable hands, *for now*," he said, adding his own caveat.

Colt stood. "In that case, I guess we should get to it."

Branch pushed to his feet. "I'll keep nudging my resources."

"I've got boots on the ground all over the county," Colt said. "I will find Sauder."

When Branch was gone, Colt went to the conference room where he'd held this morning's briefing. He surveyed the map they'd used to pinpoint the locations where citizens who belonged to the Mennonite church resided. There were four businesses. The Yoder Bakery, a furniture shop, the ironworks and a small construction company. Sauder would be well known to every single one.

He had divided the search areas into grids, but he'd left the businesses out. He planned to handle those himself. His deputies had been given a strict warning not to be pushy or intrusive. These were private people. If they said they hadn't seen Sauder or refused to answer questions, the deputy was to move on and give the name to Colt. He would take care of the more sensitive situations personally.

With a shout to his office assistant that he was heading into the field, Colt picked up his hat and made his way to the door. He might as well start with the bakery. Sarah Sauder would probably be there. Maybe he'd get lucky and her husband would show up, too.

THE BAKERY, like most of the Mennonite businesses, was just outside Winchester's town limits. Members of the community pooled their resources and purchased land whenever a desirable spot came on the market. Then the build would begin. In record time a home would be ready for occupancy or a business would be opening its doors. The Yoder Bakery was the first Mennonite business to appear in the Winchester area. Colt remembered his mother shopping there for certain cheeses. The place smelled the way his mother's kitchen had, always of some freshly baked bread or cake rising in the oven.

She'd been gone nearly thirty years now and he still missed her. Losing his dad two years ago had been even harder. He still had his two brothers but they both lived down in Alabama and he didn't see them nearly often enough.

Basically, it was just him and his son. Key had been mad as hell this morning. Having to ride the bus to school was bad enough but losing his cell phone had been like losing a limb. He'd raised holy hell but Colt had stuck to his guns. No driving and no cell phone for a whole month. The kid would survive, but he wasn't going to like a minute of it. After telling Colt how he needed a life so he would stop hyper-focusing on his, Key had called his mother. Colt had been surprised when she agreed with him. He'd almost marked the calendar hanging on the wall in the kitchen. Then again, he knew better than to trust her. She probably had a plan to undermine his authority. He just didn't know about it yet.

This wasn't the first time his son had accused him of ruining his life. Colt couldn't remember the last time he had gone on a date. Serving as sheriff kept him busy and he hadn't really wanted to…until Rey came back to town.

No use going there right now.

Colt shifted his attention back to the business at

hand and parked in the lot at the bakery. Since his truck was the only vehicle in the lot he might have a few minutes before the first customer arrived. He climbed out of the truck, scanning the area. A car was parked next to the building on the end with the side door, but it wasn't Sarah's minivan.

Work started at the bakery at about five in the morning. His stomach was already rumbling in anticipation of the aromas that would be filling the shop. Maybe he'd grab a muffin. He'd been too frustrated with Key to have breakfast this morning. Arguing with his son was the worst way to start the day.

He opened the door and the bell overhead jingled. Every shop in town seemed to have one. The scent of fresh-baked goods filled his senses. A young woman behind the counter looked up. Her brown hair was tucked into her bonnet. She smiled. "Morning, Sheriff."

Colt recognized her then. Ruby Weber. "Good morning, Ruby. Sure smells good in here. You have any of those blueberry muffins ready?"

"Sure do." She put on a pair of plastic gloves and wrapped a muffin for him.

The Mennonite women wore bonnets and modest dresses. Though they kept to themselves, he had yet to meet any member of the community who wasn't polite and helpful when asked a question.

But this time might be different. "Are Mr. and Mrs. Sauder here this morning?"

Ruby placed the muffin on the shelf above the glass case. "Afraid not, Sheriff. I imagine they're too upset to come in this morning after what happened in their home last night."

"Did Sarah let you know she wouldn't be in?" There was always the possibility that the Sauders had packed up and taken off. He'd stationed a deputy near the Yoder farm last night. Sarah and her kids had gone to her father's for the rest of the evening. The deputy hadn't seen them leave, but that didn't mean she and the kids hadn't cut across the farm on foot. Another deputy was watching the Sauder home. No activity there, either.

"She did." Ruby nodded. "She's deeply troubled about what she had to do, Sheriff. I can't imagine living with a man's blood on my hands."

"I need to talk to her, Ruby. We've learned some new information about the man who broke into her home. I'm very concerned for the safety of the Sauder family. If you speak to her again, please tell her that it's very important that she call me." He'd rather not have a meeting at her father's house, considering the man was so ill and didn't need that kind of stress. But if Sarah didn't agree to a meeting soon, he'd have no choice.

"Yes, sir. I'll sure tell her if I hear from her.

There's no phone at her daddy's place and cell service is a little hit or miss."

Not much of a guarantee.

A *ding* sounded from somewhere beyond the double swinging doors behind the counter. Ruby glanced that way. "That's my bread calling. Have a nice day, Sheriff."

"Wait, I haven't paid you for the muffin."

Ruby waved him off. "No charge for you. There's coffee if you want to take a cup with you."

Colt thanked her and watched as she disappeared through those swinging doors. He tore off a bite of muffin and popped it into his mouth. The taste exploded on his tongue. He barely restrained a groan. He'd grab a cup of coffee to go with it. Smelled fresh. There wasn't a thing in the place that didn't smell amazing.

He decided to hang around a minute while he devoured the muffin and guzzled the coffee. Might as well. Maybe Sarah would call or show up. Surely Ruby wasn't going to run the place alone.

His cell vibrated. He popped the last bite of muffin into his mouth and dragged the phone from his hip pocket. One of his deputies confirming that Sauder's minivan was still parked at her father's house.

Colt would just have to take a drive over there and see if she was still there. Maybe he was being overly suspicious. There was always the remote possibility the dead man had picked the wrong house to bust into. *Remote* being the key word in that scenario. Like Branch, Colt wasn't buying the scenario.

There was far more to the story.

He downed the last of the coffee and tossed the cup and napkin into the trash bin. Just before he reached the door, it opened, the bell jingling.

Audrey walked in. "Well, hello again, Sheriff. Looks like we're both craving the same things this morning." She reached out and dusted crumbs from his shirt.

Need, hot and fierce, clutched him. She had no idea how badly he was craving *her*. He shook off the notion. "She's not here, so don't waste your time."

Rey flashed him a smile and walked around him. "Oh my, the breakfast bars look delish."

His hand was on the door. He told himself to open it and walk out. To go on about his day and to ignore whatever Audrey was up to.

Yeah, right.

Instead, he turned around with every intention of demanding to know if she was following him. The scream that came from the back of the shop snapped his mouth shut and raised the hair on the back of his neck.

Audrey beat him around the counter and

through those swinging doors—mostly because she stepped right in front of him and he all but fell on his face trying to keep from mowing her down.

Beyond the swinging doors there was a huge kitchen. To the right was a walk-in cooler; next to it was a matching walk-in freezer. On the left there was the office and beyond that the door to the storeroom stood open; the screams were coming from there.

Audrey reached the door first but Colt was close enough to grab her by the shoulders and set her aside. He barreled through the door.

Ruby stood in the middle of the large storeroom, her face as pale as the white sacks of flour lining the shelf to the right. On the floor, leaning against the row of shelves at the back, was a man wearing black—shirt, pants, jacket—all black. His head drooped forward and the bullet that had torn through his chest had left a gaping hole via which it appeared a good portion of the blood in his body had drained, making a puddle between his spread legs.

Oh, hell.

Chapter Six

Audrey ushered Ruby away from the image of the dead man. Colt spoke quietly into his cell, calling for the necessary backup and, more than likely, the coroner. Once they were through those double doors and in the retail space of the shop, Audrey settled the shaken woman into the only chair behind the counter.

"Stay here, Ruby. I'm going to lock the door and put out the closed sign. Okay?"

She nodded, tears streaming down her face.

Then Audrey remembered she needed keys. "Where do you keep your keys?"

Ruby pointed to the register. Audrey spotted the keys, swiped them off the shelf beneath the register and hurried to the door. Once she'd locked the door, she left the keys in the lock. When the deputies and the coroner arrived someone would need to let them in.

Since she didn't spot any tissues, she grabbed a paper napkin and took it to Ruby.

"I... I should call Sarah."

"The sheriff will prefer that you don't call any-one right now, Ruby. As soon as he gives the okay, we should call your mom." Audrey wanted des-perately to go back to where Colt was, but she didn't trust Ruby to stay put. If anyone showed up at the door the rattled woman might very well let them in. "Why don't you wait in the office until Sheriff Tanner is ready to talk to you?"

Ruby stood and allowed Audrey to guide her back through those swinging doors and toward the small office they'd passed before. Once she had Ruby seated at the desk, she grabbed the cordless phone to ensure she didn't use it and patted her on the shoulder. "You stay put. I'll let the sheriff know you're waiting in the office."

Audrey was almost out the door when she had to ask. "Ruby, was the door locked when you ar-rived this morning?"

The younger woman looked up from the crum-pled napkin, her eyes glazed with worry and fear. The haze cleared and she nodded. "Yes. Yes. I had to unlock the door to come in."

"What about the back door?" Something else Audrey had noticed when she and Colt had rushed through those swinging doors. There was a back door.

Ruby scrubbed at her forehead as if digging

for the answer. "I don't know. I didn't check. I set right in to my usual routine."

"It's all right. I'm sure Sheriff Tanner will check on that."

Audrey hurried across the massive kitchen to the storeroom. She hesitated at the open door, glanced around to see if Colt was nearby, then walked right up to the body. She was careful to maintain an appropriate distance. She snapped a quick photo of the corpse, then tucked her phone back into her pocket.

If she just had her purse she could put on gloves and check the state of rigor to estimate how long he'd been dead. Blood was coagulated, looked completely dry in some areas.

"What the hell, Rey?"

She cringed at Colt's stern voice. Rather than move, she looked over at him. "He's been here several hours, maybe overnight."

Colt walked over to her, crouched down. "I can see that," he bit out. "Now let's get out of here."

She glared at him. "We're already here. A minute won't change the fact that we both walked into the primary scene."

When he opened his mouth to argue with her, she went on, "You have gloves on." She nodded to the latex he'd pulled over his hands. "Check his fingers and then his arms."

Jaw clenched, eyes shooting daggers at her, he

reached for the dead man's fingers. They moved easily. "Loose." Then he tried moving the arm, bending the elbow. "Still rigid."

"He's been dead overnight. Twelve or more hours." She'd seen enough bodies and interviewed enough medical examiners to have a reasonably good handle on how things worked the first twenty-four or so hours after death.

Another of those glares arrowed in her direction. "Let's go, Rey."

This time she didn't argue. She had what she needed to know. This guy had probably died around the same time or a little before the one in Sarah Sauder's kitchen. Considering this bakery belonged to Sarah's family as well, finding yet another gunshot victim turned the case in a whole different direction.

When they were outside the storeroom, she mentioned, "Ruby said the front door was locked when she came in. But she didn't check the back." Audrey glanced in the direction of the rear exit.

"Were you questioning her? Damn it, Rey." His long-fingered hands bracketed his waist. "You need to wait out front. Sit your butt on that bench and just wait until I tell you to move."

Like that was going to happen. "Please. Arrest me or throw me out, but do not tell me what to do, Colt Tanner."

"Fine. Audrey Anderson, you are under arrest for interfering with an investigation."

He removed a pair of cuffs from the hip pocket of his jeans. Her jaw dropped in disbelief. "You cannot arrest me, Colt Tanner. I walked into this establishment like any other customer. I cannot be held responsible for what happened after that."

"Give me any more grief and I'll add resisting arrest." Fury radiated from him like heat from a roaring fire.

He was serious.

She held out her hands and he snapped the cuffs on her wrists, all the while reciting her rights as if she were an actual criminal. It wasn't the first time she'd been hauled away from a crime scene in iron bracelets. It was just the first time Colt Tanner had dared to defy her.

How the hell had that happened?

Long fingers wrapped around her upper arm and he guided her through the bakery's swinging doors and to the bench beyond the counter. "Now sit. And don't say one word."

When he'd disappeared into the back once more, Audrey reached into her pocket for her cell, iron bracelets clinking. Colt was going to regret this. She punched the contact for Brian and pressed the phone to her ear.

"Where are you? I've put off the staff meeting."

"I'm at Yoder Bakery," she whispered. If Colt

heard her on the phone he would take it from her. "There's another body."

"Oh my God. Who?"

"Don't know. I took a photo. I'm sending it to you."

"Colt will have a—"

"We're not printing it. The photo is for ID purposes only. Strictly between you and me."

"Why are you whispering?" Brian whispered back.

"Colt arrested me for interfering in an investigation. Looks like the guy has been dead since around the same time as what's-his-name who Sarah Sauder shot." What the hell was the guy's name? "Marcello. Tony Marcello."

"Wait, wait, wait. Colt arrested you. Are you serious?"

Audrey glanced toward the doors, blew out a breath of exasperation. "As a heart attack."

"I'll be right there." Brian was no longer whispering. He was damned near shouting.

"No," Audrey ordered as loudly as she dared. "Focus on ID'ing the dead guy. I'm okay. I have to go."

Brian was still speaking when she ended the call. Keeping an eye on the doors, she tapped the photo and sent it to Brian via text. The dead man was dressed the same as the other one, black pants and shirt, but his black jacket was a hoodie. He looked a good deal younger than the other guy as well. Was he shot before or after Marcello? Maybe this guy explained why Wesley Sauder never came home.

Audrey tucked her phone away. The sound of engines outside had her turning around on the bench. Two deputy cruisers and the coroner's van skidded to stops in the parking lot. Burt must have been on his way to the clinic. He was never this quick on the draw. She glanced at the door. Might as well let them in.

She pushed to her feet and went to the glass door and twisted the key. The door was yanked open, setting the bell above it into a stunted tune. Audrey stepped back to prevent being trampled by four men in tan and brown uniforms. The last of the four nodded and said, "Morning, Ms. Anderson."

James Carter's son. The Carter family had run the local hardware store for five generations. The one just off the downtown square, Mr. Carter would remind her, not the big-box place on the boulevard.

"Morning," she replied.

It was Burt who stopped and stared at her shackled state. "What in the world?"

"Colt's mad at me," she confessed.

Burt's eyes widened behind his glasses. "Did you shoot someone, Rey?"

"No." She glanced toward the back of the bakery. "But I might before this is over."

"Burt!"

They both turned at the sound of Colt's voice.

"What's the holdup?"

"Gotta go!" Burt shuffled away, skirting the counter and hurrying toward the door where Colt waited.

The sheriff didn't so much as glance at Audrey before disappearing once more.

The sound of tires squealing drew her attention back to the big window where handmade posters boasted today's specials, including peanut butter balls—buy four, get two free. Her mouth watered despite the circumstances. The van that squealed to a stop belonged to the *Tullahoma Telegraph*. Audrey locked the door and hurried behind the racks of baked goods. When she felt confident no one outside could see her, she relaxed. Annalise Guthrie was the dauntless reporter who liked trumping Audrey's stories.

"Not today, honey," Audrey muttered.

Her cell vibrated. She dragged it from her pocket and checked the screen. Brian. "Hey. What'd you find?"

"Casey Pranno. Guess where he's from—"

"He works with Marcello?"

"You know it. I spoke to Wanda Mulberry over at the post office not five minutes ago when I dropped off the mail. If any new marshals have shown up she would know, since Branch's office is in the same building. No new faces yet, but she did say Branch had just torn out of there. She saw him bust out the front entrance and hustle out to his truck. He'll probably be there any second."

No sooner had Brian said the words, than two deputies hurried through the swinging doors and to the front entrance. After unlocking it they pushed out. Audrey didn't have to sneak a look to know they would be setting the perimeter and shooing the other reporter outside the set boundary.

"Put together a background piece on Marcello and Pranno. If we have nothing else, we'll run that on tomorrow's front page, but hold the presses as long as possible."

The tinkle of the bell warned that someone was coming in. "Gotta go."

Audrey slid her phone back into her pocket and craned her neck to see who stepped beyond the racks blocking her view of the door.

Branch glanced left, then right, spotted Audrey and automatically removed his hat. "Rey, you hiding over there?"

She moved a few steps closer but not close enough to be spotted via telescopic lenses peering in through the glass front of the shop. If Annalise was out there, there would be others. She waved her hands. "Colt arrested me for interfering with his investigation."

Branch shook his head and walked over to where she stood. "Has he lost his mind?" He reached into his pocket, withdrew a key and released her. "You must have really ticked him off."

She rubbed her wrists. "I might have."

But he deserved it. She could tick him off every day for the rest of his life and it would never be repayment enough for what he had done to her. All the details she kept to herself. Branch had been in college by the time she and Colt broke up, but he'd likely heard the rumors.

Branch grinned. "You always were a feisty one."

He had no idea. The image of that cold, damp basement beneath the newspaper flitted through her head. "I'll take that as a compliment."

"Come on." He jerked his head toward the counter. "We'll see what Sheriff Tanner has to say when I tell him I'm taking custody of his prisoner."

Audrey couldn't help herself—she smiled. "One of these days you two are going to have to put your gridiron days behind you."

"I doubt that's going to happen before one or both of us is laid out for visitation over at DuPont Funeral Home."

Like the family newspaper, DuPont Funeral

Home was one of the oldest establishments in Winchester. Though Branch meant that remark as a joke, Audrey couldn't laugh. DuPont had taken care of her father after he died. She had no desire to see anyone else she cared about inside that old Victorian house–turned–funeral home.

The thought of the spooky old place made her shudder.

"You cold, Rey?" he asked as he ushered her through the swinging doors.

"I'm good. Thank you."

She heard the muffled sound of that bell over the entrance door again and two more uniforms crowded into the bakery kitchen. These two she recognized from last night. The evidence techs.

"I should probably stay over here," she said to Branch when he started for the storeroom door.

He gave her a nod and moved on. Audrey was perfectly content to watch. If she leaned forward ever so slightly she could see Colt in the office with Ruby. She could imagine the poor woman was terrified.

Pies prepared for sliding into the ovens lined the stainless counter of one table. Audrey stepped back to ensure she was not in view of the office door and snapped a photo of the pies. The dusting of flour on the shiny steel provided a perfect back-drop to the pies. It wasn't the sort of grisly photo she generally took at a crime scene, but this was a Southern small town. Readers would eat this up.

Having been caught in situations like this before, she sent the photo to her email, then deleted both it and the one of the dead man from her phone. Colt would want to check her phone. While she was at it, she deleted the calls to and from Brian. Feeling cocky, she leaned against the wall next to the sink a few feet from the swinging doors. On the wall above the sink was another handmade sign. This one ordered employees to wash their hands before waiting on customers and then again when returning to the kitchen.

She wondered if Wesley Sauder had come to the bakery and found himself face-to-face with the man lying on the floor in the storeroom, while his wife was being visited by the man she'd shot in her kitchen.

If Sauder was dead, his wife would likely say so.

He was in hiding, Audrey would bet. Somehow he had crossed the mob and they were after him. It wasn't necessary to be a cop to know that whoever sent these guys wouldn't stop until he achieved his goal. If anyone in local law enforcement had any doubts, they should be fully convinced now.

Colt came out of the office. His gaze landed on her and his lips tightened. She noticed when she examined his face for tells. He was still angry.

He strode over to her. "What the hell are you doing back here?"

She held up her hands. "Branch uncuffed me and brought me back here. He told me to wait in this spot and I've been doing exactly that." Before Colt could open his mouth and unleash the storm of fury whirling in his eyes, she added, "There are reporters out front. He didn't want any of them to see me."

He certainly couldn't deny the validity of the excuse. Instead, he grabbed her by the arm. "Come with me."

She blinked. Before she could demand what he meant, he executed an about-face and strode to the door marked Employees Only. She followed. Once inside the cramped bathroom, he shut the door.

"Are you trying to get on my last nerve?"

Maybe the bad night he'd had was making his temper flare so easily. The Colt she knew was generally far more patient than this.

"I am not. I was here for a scone. To my knowledge that isn't against the law." He didn't have to know she'd stopped in hopes of seeing Sarah. "When Ruby screamed, we both ran to where she was." She shrugged. "And you arrested me. I'm a victim of circumstance."

He plowed a hand though his hair, reminding her of all the times she used to do that.

Stop.

"I'm sorry I took my frustration out on you." He heaved a big breath. "But you shouldn't have gone into that storeroom. You went too far, Rey."

"His name is Casey Pranno. He was an associate of Mr. Marcello's—the other dead guy."

Colt closed his eyes for a second, shook his head. "Please tell me you did not take a picture of that man's body and send it to anyone."

Okay, so she had no choice but to tell him. "Only to Brian. We're not printing it. I've already deleted it from my phone."

"You swear to me, Rey. Swear right now that you will not print that photo."

If he hadn't sounded and looked so damned desperate she might have made him beg a little more. "I swear, Colt. You know me better than that. I would never disrespect your office." She shrugged again. "Not unless you made me by leaving me out and blocking my efforts to do *my* job."

"Okay." Another big breath deflated his lungs. "You can go now if you like."

"You mean I'm not under arrest?"

He glanced at the ceiling.

"I didn't tell Branch what I just told you."

Looking down at her, he held her gaze for a moment that lapsed into two. And in that extra second she felt the heat and desire for him that she had not felt since that first time he kissed her in eighth grade.

"Thank you."

She nodded, uncertain of her voice.

"You can go out the back to avoid the reporters."

"Won't do any good." She'd only just realized this part. "My car is out front."

Her vanity plate read PAPRGRL. Everyone knew who drove that car.

"All right. You can stay back here but stick to that sink over there like it's your long-lost best friend. Do not move from that spot."

"I won't."

He reached for the door, the move putting his face so very close to hers.

"As long as you give me an exclusive sound bite," she added.

He turned, looked directly at her, practically nose to nose. "I'll give you whatever you want, Rey. I always have."

And then he was gone.

She leaned against the wall, had to wait until her heart stopped pounding before she moved.

She was not, *was not* going to get tangled up with Colt Tanner again.

Never, ever, ever.

Chapter Seven

Colt pulled loose the posted warning that proclaimed the Sauder house to be a crime scene and folded it in half. He used the key that belonged to Sarah to unlock the front door of her home. Both the Sauder home and the bakery were now crime scenes. He walked into the house and turned on the overhead light. It was late afternoon with plenty of daylight left, but the windows were darkened with curtains and sheers.

Though this wasn't the first time in his career he'd had murder scenes to investigate two days in a row, it was the first time both scenes had belonged to the same family. He moved around the living room. A sofa sat on one side of the room; a couple of rockers flanked the fireplace. Not much else in the way of furnishings or decor. There was an old rotary phone on one of the side tables. The few Mennonites who had phones were the ones who were business owners. Most didn't care for the bothersome devices. A walk through the four bedrooms revealed the same: beds with plain linens, a chest with drawers—most of which were empty—and a few modest garments hanging in the tiny closets.

Each room in the house had been searched and scrutinized for evidence not once, but twice. There was nothing here that seemed connected to the dead man or Chicago and certainly not to organized crime. The one bathroom in the house revealed even less. Homemade soap and shampoo, towels hanging over the rim of the tub. There was a straight razor, a comb and a brush. Beyond the place on the wood floor where the small pool of blood had left its stain, the kitchen offered only the necessities. Pots and pans, the dishes and glassware in the cabinets. A well-stocked pantry. One drawer held a couple of tablecloths. Another was packed with hand towels and oven mitts. None of the fingerprints taken from the home were found in any databases. Made sense, since the dead guy had been wearing gloves.

Colt checked the back door. The victim had entered the home through that door. The lock was a piece of cake for even an amateur burglar. A guy like Marcello likely unlocked the door with his eyes closed and one hand behind his back. Colt had suggested Sarah have a dead bolt installed. If her husband wasn't handy with a drill and a screwdriver, Colt felt confident one of her brothers could handle the job.

After locking up and taking a walk around the yard, he loaded in his truck and headed for the Yoder place. He would talk to her again, see if she'd suddenly remembered anything she was too upset to recall last night. Colt didn't see any reason not to release her house. His evidence technicians had searched the house thoroughly, including checking for loose floorboards and hidden nooks in the walls, the crawl space and the attic. There was nothing useful to the investigation in the Sauder home. Whatever secrets they were keeping, they'd left nothing for anyone to find.

Melvin Yoder's farm was barely two miles down the road. The house sat on a rise overlooking pastures in front. Cows grazed, barely noticing as Colt turned onto the long drive. Behind the house, fields already prepared for crops extended for as far as the eye could see. Beyond all that were the woods. Yoder owned hundreds of acres. His name was well known throughout the county. He had a reputation for honesty and kindness. Would he have taken in a man with connections to organized crime?

Not knowingly, Colt was certain. He'd heard rumors of a falling-out between Yoder and Sauder, but so far no one had confirmed as much. Maybe this afternoon he'd learn the whole story. After talking to Sarah, he needed to stop by the bakery and check on the progress his evidence techs were making. Then he'd need to follow up with Branch. He wasn't about to let Branch get too far ahead of him or leave him out of the loop in this investigation.

He thought about how Branch had removed Audrey's handcuffs this morning. Colt had always suspected that Branch liked her. He really didn't have any right to be jealous or to begrudge the other man a shot at a relationship with Audrey. But the thought tore him apart inside.

Colt parked behind the minivan that belonged to Sarah Sauder. He got out of his truck and shut the door. The chickens pecking at insects around the yard raised their heads and eyed him speculatively. The dog stretched out on the front porch didn't bother lifting its head, but its tail swept back and forth across the worn wood. Colt remembered the dog as a pup from his first weeks in the department as a brand-new eager deputy. He and his father had stopped by to offer their condolences when Mrs. Yoder passed away. Pepper had to be fifteen or sixteen years old now. No wonder she didn't bother getting up.

Before he took his first step toward the house, his cell vibrated in his hip pocket. He tugged it out, hoping like hell it wasn't another murder. *Key* flashed on the screen. Colt sighed and paused to take the call from his son. "What's up?"

"How am I supposed to get home from school?"

It wasn't quite three yet, but the dismissal bell would be ringing any minute. "Take the bus."

"No way."

The shock in the two words reverberated loud and clear across the airwaves. Key hadn't ridden the school bus since he was in third grade and it was the thing to do with all his friends. After that, his mother or Colt had taken him to school and picked him up until he was sixteen and started driving himself. At almost eighteen, the bus was so not cool.

Too bad.

"Like I told you this morning, take the bus or walk."

Colt had given him strict orders about transportation. No going anywhere in a vehicle with his friends. No rides to and from school from his mom or Colt. He rode the bus or he walked. End of story.

The call ended.

Colt shook his head. Part of him felt like a heel for being so hard on the kid, but the cop in him knew better than to ignore the warning signs of trouble. If he got away with drinking and driving now, it would only get worse later. The idea that his son could have killed himself or someone else last night terrified Colt.

Damn his ex for allowing the boy to run wild. Damn him for letting her do it. Watching his son stagger across the yard had been a serious wake-up call.

The chill in the morning air was long gone. The afternoon sun was beating down as if it were summer already instead of the final days of winter. But then that was life in the South.

He climbed the steps and crossed the porch. A pot of tulips not quite ready to bloom sat next to the door. Melvin's wife had been dead for years now. Sarah probably kept her mother's flowers going. Melvin Yoder didn't seem like the type to plant or weed flowers. Then again, when a man loved a woman so much, he might do most anything to keep the things that meant something to her going.

Colt would never tell a soul, but he kept all the things he'd given Rey and the things she'd given him in the closet of his room, including the locket he gave her when they were thirteen. After they broke up, she'd packed up every single gift he'd ever given her and shipped them back. Her momma could have dropped it off if Rey didn't want to, but he'd figured she wanted to make a statement by using a delivery service. There was something final about getting that box delivered by a stranger.

He'd opened the box a hundred times over the years.

"Kind of pathetic, Colt," he muttered as he raised his fist and rapped on the wood frame of the screen door.

It was quiet beyond the door. He'd been in Melvin's house before, when he was a teenager. No television. There had been a radio but it hadn't been turned on at the time. Colt had come with his daddy to tell the family that their younger daughter, Bethany, was in the hospital after a drug overdose.

Bethany had survived but her relationship with her family hadn't. She'd ended up taking off for Nashville to try making it as a country music singer. Truth was, she was pretty good. But Music City had been hard on her. Eventually she'd shown up back in Winchester waitressing at one bar or another.

No one in her family had spoken to her since the day she left town, fifteen years ago. She was thirty-one now, just a couple of years younger than Sarah. Living in Winchester and totally ostracized from her family had to be tough.

The door opened and Aaron Yoder stood on the other side of the screen door. Colt sure hated to do this at Melvin's house but the second murder and Sarah's avoidance pretty much left him out of options.

"Afternoon, Sheriff," he said. "You here to see Sarah?"

Colt nodded. "I figured she was home." He jerked his head toward the driveway and her parked van. "Is Wesley here?"

Aaron's jaw tightened—just a little, but Colt noticed. "No, sir. He's not here. You want to come in and talk to Sarah? She just got the children down for a nap."

Colt grimaced. "I don't want to disturb the kids. She could sit on the porch with me a few minutes if she doesn't mind."

"No need. The children are in the back bedroom." Aaron reached to open the screen door; Colt stepped back. "Come on in."

"Thanks." Colt crossed the threshold, removed his hat and glanced around. "How's your daddy?"

"Not too good," Aaron admitted as he closed the door. "He sleeps a lot now. They say that's normal at this stage."

Cancer was an ugly disease. "I hope all this business at Sarah's house and at the bakery hasn't been too hard on him."

"He doesn't want to talk about it, so I let it go."

"Sheriff."

Aaron's posture stiffened at the sound of his sister's voice. Definite tension.

"I'm sorry to have to bother you again, Sarah. But I need to ask you a few more questions in light of what we found at the bakery this morning."

She nodded once. "Come into the sitting room, Sheriff. You want some water? I have lemonade, too."

"No, thank you, ma'am."

"I need to check on Poppa," Aaron said before disappearing down the hall.

When Sarah had settled on the couch, Colt sat down in one of the chairs flanking a table. "Sarah, I really do need to speak with your husband. Can you tell me how to find him?"

She turned her hands up. "With all that's happened, he's going door-to-door reassuring everyone that we've nothing to fear."

"Sarah, does your husband know either of the men who were killed on your property?"

She moved her head side to side. "He surely does not. We believe the one who broke into our home killed the other man in the bakery and then came to our house. There has to be some kind of mistake. We don't know these men or why they've come all this way to do whatever it is they intended to do."

"You know your husband lived near Chicago and both these men are from Chicago. They worked together, so I'm not inclined to believe they just drove down to Tennessee to kill each other."

A shrug lifted her cotton-clad shoulders. "I sure don't know what to tell you, Sheriff. We're as confused as you are."

"Sarah." He leaned forward, braced his forearms on his knees, his hat in his hands. "Whatever these men are after, the people who sent them won't stop just because the first round of their soldiers has been taken care of. There will be others. If you or your husband knows of some reason they want to hurt your family, you need to share that information with me. It could mean the difference between life and death."

She shook her head again. "Good gracious, Sheriff. Why would they want to hurt us? We're just common people. Serve the Lord. We sure don't have anything valuable but our children and our souls."

"Sarah, is it true that Wesley and your father had a falling-out a few months ago?"

She made a face. "Where on earth did you hear a thing like that? My poppa thinks the world of Wesley. You should know that, Sheriff. You were raised here. You know how much Wesley helped Poppa. My brothers were all so young and couldn't do the things that needed to be done. We would have had an awfully hard time without Wesley."

"Is there any reason for you to believe that your father or one of your brothers knows these men?"

"Lord have mercy, no. My brothers and I might

not always get along but they would never be involved in trouble. We don't break the law."

"I wish I could make you understand how important it is that I speak with Wesley." An idea occurred to Colt. "We're worried that these two hit men may have your husband confused with someone else. I can't help him if he doesn't talk to me. This is a very serious situation, Sarah. It's not going to just go away."

"Sheriff, I'm afraid you're barking up the wrong tree. Wesley and I are the victims here. Someone came into our home and our bakery. Two men are dead. It's an awful thing, but it has nothing to do with us."

Colt wished he could believe her story. "You and your whole family are in danger because of this, Sarah. I need to speak to Wesley."

"I'll try to find him," she promised. "I'll tell him how badly you need to talk to him. Maybe he can make time."

Colt stood. "I sure appreciate your cooperation, Sarah. Please give your daddy my regards."

She nodded and looked away as if the mention of her father pained her somehow. Well, he was dying. One estranged daughter in the family was more than enough. Obviously, Sarah didn't want her relationship with her father to end that way.

Sarah followed Colt to the door. "Did you find

anything in the bakery that will tell you what happened, Sheriff?"

The way she phrased the question, as if she already knew the answer and just wanted to see if he did, made him want to fire a dozen more questions at her.

"Not yet, but we're working on it. We're hoping the victims' cell phones will give us some answers." He stood on the porch, settled his hat into place. "Be sure to tell Wesley I need to talk to him as soon as possible."

"I'll let him know," she called after Colt.

He had a feeling he wouldn't have an opportunity to talk to Wesley Sauder until he hunted him down and handcuffed him to a chair.

The metal bracelets hanging on his belt made him think of snapping them onto Rey's wrists. Somehow he needed to get it through her head that this investigation could turn into a very dangerous situation. He wanted to protect her.

Before he called it a day, he would be following up with her. Whether she wanted his protection or not, he needed to keep close tabs on her or she would be eyeball-deep in the trouble he suspected was about to descend on his county.

Who was he kidding? She already was.

Chapter Eight

Happy Kids Daycare Center was established nine years ago by Happy Jennings. According to Audrey's mother—before dementia stole so many of her memories—Happy graduated from high school and went to nursing school in Tullahoma at Motlow College. She tried the nursing field working at the hospital and then a local doctor's office. But Happy was never *happy* working with the sick and the injured—never mind the dying. So she started a day care center and it was a big hit. All the mothers who had made fun of Happy all through school, primarily laughing at her name, were thrilled to have someone watching over their offspring all day who was also a registered nurse.

Now, nine years later, Happy was the administrator over a dozen employees. Happy Kids had won numerous awards from the Chamber of Commerce as well as the city of Winchester. Who was laughing now?

Happy Kids was a bright yellow building that

had once been a church right off the square in downtown Winchester. The fenced yard was dotted with colorful swings and slides and sandboxes. Audrey opened the gate and made her way to the entrance. Tulips and daffodils filled the window boxes and the pots on either side of the door. At this hour, half past five, most folks had picked up their little ones. According to the sign on the front door, the center closed at six.

Beyond the door, a reception area was empty. Like the exterior, the walls were a bright yellow with clouds on the ceiling and multicolored linoleum tiles on the floor. A door across the room opened and a young woman, all smiles but looking a bit harried, entered the lobby.

"Hello. May I help you?"

An employee. Great. "Hi, I'd like to see Happy if she's available."

"Her office is right down that hall." The woman pointed to a narrow hall on the far west side of the room.

Audrey thanked her and headed that way. Once she was in the hall, she understood why Happy's office was this way. Large windows overlooking the shared interior play area were on one side while windows to the outside play area were on the other. Ingenious. A handful of children were running around the inside play area, laughing and trying to be the one who got the bright red ball next. Around the perimeter of the play area were doors and more large windows; beyond each window was what appeared to be an individual classroom. Happy's office, the entire wall facing the hall made of glass, had the perfect view into the play area and classrooms.

Ideal setup.

Happy spotted Audrey before she could rap on the glass door. She motioned for her to come on in. With a pointed look at Audrey's flat abdomen, she asked, "Are you here to preregister?" Happy gestured to a blue chair in front of her desk. "We do have extensive waiting lists. Most mothers sign their kids up before they're born. You're smart to come in now."

It wasn't until she said the last that Audrey realized Happy thought she was pregnant. "Oh no." She waved her hands back and forth. "No babies in my future."

Whether it was her words echoing in the room or the other woman's pained expression, Audrey suddenly felt hollow. She drew in a sharp breath and forced the ridiculous reaction aside. She didn't have a significant other at the moment; how could she be having a baby anyway? Audrey felt reasonably confident raising a child was far easier with a partner.

"Oh!" Happy laughed her trademark cackle and shook her head. "I'm sorry. It's just that most people who drop in…" She shook her head again. "Anyway, how are you? You look fantastic! Being back home agrees with you, Rey."

Audrey relaxed, though the uneasy feeling lingered despite her efforts to dismiss it. "I'm glad to be home. Close to Mom. Taking care of the paper."

Happy's expression shifted to one of concern. "How is your mother?"

"She has her good days and her bad ones." There was always that question.

Everyone who'd grown up in Winchester knew the Andersons. The name was synonymous with news. Audrey didn't need to ask to know her mother likely spent the past decade or so raving about her world-traveling daughter always in the headlines of some big paper. Mary Jo Anderson made it sound as if Audrey was some big celebrity whose life was filled with awards, exotic locations and excitement. The awards came, that was true. And there had been plenty of excitement and great locations. But there had also been loneliness and the ever-nagging sense of regret.

What if she'd stayed home; could she have helped her mother more? Would she be married now with children to bring to Happy's day care center?

Would she and Colt have worked things out?

Shock radiated through Audrey and she blinked,

that last thought startling her more deeply than anything had recently—even finding a dead man in the storeroom of her favorite bakery.

"Don't we all," Happy mused. "But the bad days often remind us how lucky we are on the good days." She sighed. "So, to what do I owe the pleasure of your visit, Rey? You know you have always been one of my favorite people. The nicest girl in school."

Audrey smiled. "If I recall, there was a time when you and Aaron Yoder were an item of sorts."

Happy's expression shifted to something slightly less than happy. "You're looking into the murders. I heard about the other dead man they found at the bakery."

"I am." Audrey shook her head. "I just can't see Sarah shooting one man, much less two."

"I guess any of us could if he broke into our house or place of business and threatened us or our children."

That much was true. "There are some who believe Sarah might be covering for one of her brothers. Maybe Aaron." This part was pure conjecture. Audrey had overhead one of the deputies make a comment to that effect.

Happy's face changed again. Shock claimed her expression, and the slightest hint of anger glinted in her eyes. "That is the most ridiculous thing I have ever heard." Outrage weighted her tone.

"Aaron would never shoot anyone unless they shot at him first. Were those dead guys armed? Did they fire their weapons first? Where in the world did you hear such a thing?"

"No indication either of them fired first." Unless the bullets had lodged inside someone—like Wesley Sauder or one of the brothers. There were no bullets or casings found at the scene. This she knew for a certainty. No word yet on whether either of the victims' weapons had been fired. If the lab had confirmed as much, Colt was holding back that information.

Happy shook her head adamantly. "I am telling you right now, Rey, he couldn't do this. Aaron is the most tenderhearted man on this planet. He would never hurt anyone unless he had no choice."

"Are you and Aaron still friends?" As the other woman's expression closed, Audrey hastened to add, "I'm not here to cause Aaron any trouble. I want to help him. This is what I do, Happy. I have traveled the world, like my mom said. I've done all sorts of stories, but I'm most known for the ones that bring the truth to light. This is not my first murder investigation."

Happy shrugged. "Your momma always said you were a hero to a lot of people in a lot of stories."

Okay, that might be stretching things a bit, but mothers had a tendency to brag. "I do what I can.

If there's anything you can do to help me help Aaron, I'm sure he will appreciate it in the long run."

"Aaron hasn't mentioned anything like this," she countered, unknowingly admitting to exactly what Audrey wanted to hear.

"Is there a problem between him and Sarah or between Sarah and their father?"

Happy stared at her desk for a moment, likely weighing how far she wanted to go with what she knew or suspected. No matter that she and Aaron could never have a life together; she still cared about him. That was the Happy Audrey knew. Loyal to the bone.

"Whatever you tell me will remain in confidence," Audrey assured her. "I'll use the information to help find the truth, but I'm not going to report what you tell me. You have my word."

"Sarah and her daddy had a big argument about two months ago. Melvin learned some disturbing information about Wesley, Sarah's husband. He was very upset about all of it."

"Do you know what sort of information he discovered?" Audrey was practically on the edge of her seat. There had to be a connection between Wesley Sauder and one or both of the dead guys. One so-called button man might make a mistake and show up at the wrong place, but two different men making the same mistake? Not likely.

"He wouldn't say." She shrugged. "Maybe his daddy didn't give him all the details. Either way he wouldn't talk about what the problem was. He only said that Wesley Sauder was not the man they had all thought he was. You know, that could mean anything. I did see bruises on Sarah's arms once. She claimed she fell and hurt herself, but I didn't believe her. But I've never seen anything but good out of Wesley. Goodness sakes, he was always doing for others. Spearheading every build in their community, helping the businesses to thrive. His work even crossed over to our community. None of this makes sense."

"Do you know Wesley beyond what you've heard from others about him?"

She shook her head. "Not really. I mean, I know him when I see him, but he's not the sort who associates with you unless it somehow benefits his cause. Aaron told me he didn't waste his time on people who don't matter. But if you talk to anyone else, they'll tell you what a good man he is, how he helps everyone."

It sounded as if Aaron was definitely not a fan of his brother-in-law. And Happy was torn between her loyalty to Aaron and the reputation Wesley Sauder had garnered for himself.

"What makes Aaron so unsure of Wesley?"

"You know, he has never really said a whole lot about him. But he did remind me that Wesley just happened to come along at the same time that old bull charged Melvin and injured him so badly. Aaron said he never could understand what made the bull charge. He never had before. At the time, they were all so grateful Wesley was able to get Melvin out of the pasture and to the hospital that no one asked any questions. Looking back, I have to agree with Aaron—it seems awfully convenient that he came along on that deserted road at exactly the right time."

"Why would Mr. Yoder put so much support behind Wesley in the community rather than one of his own sons?" This part truly puzzled Audrey.

"In part, I suppose, because he was older," Happy offered. "Aaron and his brothers were all so young back then. By the time they were old enough, Wesley was the person everyone looked up to. It was too late to change what was done."

"Would Aaron or any of his brothers protect Wesley? Help him hide from the police or a threat of some sort? Like those two men who showed up and broke in?"

Happy shook her head slowly from side to side. "No way. They dislike him intensely. Wesley would never go to one of them."

Well, well, there it was. "Does Aaron have any idea where his brother-in-law might hide out?"

"If they knew, I'm pretty sure one of them would find a way to get word to Colt." Happy looked beyond Audrey at the wall of windows across the narrow hall. "The trouble is, it could be anyone in the Mennonite community—besides them—hiding Wesley. They all love him. He's like the messiah or some celebrity."

"Is there any possibility that Aaron or one of his brothers handled the situation?" Audrey pressed the other woman with her gaze. "If Wesley was causing problems for the family, this situation would be the perfect time to get rid of him and allow the world to think another one of those guys from Chicago took care of him."

Happy was shaking her head again. "They would never do that. Never. You have to believe me on that one, Rey. They're not like that. The Yoder boys—men—are good, kind souls. They couldn't kill anyone. I'm not even sure they could or would kill someone to protect themselves. More likely they'd just injure the attacker real bad."

"Not even if their daddy told them to take care of Wesley?"

She laughed then, but there was no humor in the sound. "Melvin Yoder would never go against God that way. He would sooner sacrifice himself than someone else. If there was ever a man born without a mean bone in his body, it was Melvin Yoder."

This was getting Audrey nowhere. She needed to know where to look. "Is there someone in the

Mennonite community who would be more likely to hide Wesley? Maybe someone Aaron mentioned as being a particularly close friend of his brother-in-law's?"

Happy considered the question for a moment. "Ezra Zimmerman. He and Wesley are tight, according to Aaron."

Finally, there was a piece of information she needed. "Thanks, Happy. I appreciate your candor."

Audrey stood; the other woman did the same. "So you know, Colt asked me pretty much the same questions."

"He did?"

Happy nodded. "Couple of hours ago."

"Did you tell him what you told me?"

"No. I was actually going to drop by the newspaper after I closed the center to talk to you. No offense to Colt, but he's following the law. If I was going to help Aaron and his family, I wanted someone who was going to follow their heart. I know you'll do that, Rey."

Audrey smiled. "I owe you one, Happy."

"A nice half-page ad about our upcoming registration might be nice."

"You've got it. I'll have Brian contact you."

Audrey left the Happy Kids Daycare Center and drove straight to Ezra Zimmerman's dairy farm. The wife and two children were home, but not Ezra. His wife had no idea when he would be home, and she had not seen or spoken to Wesley Sauder. She thought her husband might be home later that night.

Since it would be dark soon, Audrey decided to drive back to the paper. She would check in with Brian and let him know her plan. She was staking out the Zimmerman place for the night. She'd need binoculars, water and snacks. Toilet paper for trips into the woods across the road.

Most important, she needed to borrow Brian's black car. Her silver one wasn't so good for hiding.

"I THINK I should do this with you," Brian insisted as she slid behind the wheel of his compact black two-door sports car.

"One of us has to put the paper to bed, and that's you." She started the engine. "I have my cell, a charger, water and snacks." And the toilet paper. All of which was in the minuscule back seat. Was a human really supposed to ride back there?

He heaved a disgusted sigh. "Fine, but if anything happens to you, just know that I'll feel guilty for the rest of my life. How can you do that to a friend?"

Audrey laughed. "But you can say I told you so."

"Just be careful. I don't want you to end up like those two interlopers."

"I will be very careful. Don't forget about that ad space for Happy's center. I promised her you would take care of it personally."

"I'll take care of it. You just take care of you."

She gave him a thumbs-up, and when she would have shifted into Drive and pulled away, Colt's truck parked next to her.

She looked from the big black truck to the man standing outside the window of her driver's-side door. "Tell me you did not call him."

Brian held up his hands. "I swear I did not call him."

Colt opened the passenger-side door and dropped into the passenger seat of Brian's car. He pulled off his hat and placed it in the back seat on top of her supplies. "Ready?"

She glowered first at him, then at her trusted friend and employee. She powered up her window and shifted into Drive. "What're you doing here, Colt?"

As she rolled away from the newspaper parking lot, he tugged on his seat belt and made himself comfortable by powering the seat back as far as possible, which was not very far. She was surprised his long legs fit into the vehicle, much less the rest of his lean, hard body.

Dear God, stop with the physical details already!

"Keeping you out of trouble, Rey," he said in answer to her question.

She glanced at him as she pointed the car toward their destination. "I'm not in trouble, Colt."

"Not for a lack of trying," he grumbled.

"Did Brian call you?" She couldn't believe he had lied to her—straight to her face.

"He did not."

"Happy, then?" Why hadn't Happy just told Colt about Ezra in the first place? Damn her.

"I said Brian didn't call me. I didn't say he didn't tell me."

Fury tightened Audrey's lips. "He sent you a text."

"Three," Colt confirmed. "One: 'you gotta get over here, Colt.'"

She was going to have a very long, very unpleasant conversation with Brian.

"Two: 'she is planning a stakeout tonight.'"

Audrey put her anger on pause. "What about the third one?"

"'I'm worried she might need backup.'"

A grin spread across her face. "So he didn't tell you where I was going?"

FIVE HOURS LATER there hadn't been any movement at the Zimmerman place. Ezra's truck had been parked in the driveway when they arrived and it still was. The lights had gone out about ten. Colt was happy she was prepared for the stakeout. She had chips and her favorite chocolate bars, which happened to be his favorite as well. They'd binged on the junk food the way they had back in high school, but they washed it down with water rather than colas.

Still, she would be sorry tomorrow.

"This wife is his second one?" Audrey asked. Her mother had mentioned Mrs. Zimmerman dying a few years back. If memory served, the Zimmermans didn't have children. But there had been a really young woman, maybe midtwenties, and two children when Audrey knocked on the door. The woman had said she was Ezra's wife.

"Yep. His first wife died a while back, maybe five or six years ago. They had been married since they were teenagers. He married again about three years ago and had two kids."

"Living alone gets to you sometimes. It's probably really difficult after spending your whole adult life with someone and then finding yourself alone."

The words echoed in the confined space and Audrey flinched in the darkness. That was one admission she would have preferred to keep to herself. She certainly hadn't intended to say it aloud to Colt. "Mom said that to me a couple of times," she amended, her words tumbling over one another. "You know, before I came back home."

He was silent for a while. Surprisingly, sitting in the dark with him was easy. She didn't feel the usual tension that accompanied being within a dozen yards of him. Maybe it was not being able to see his face or those gray eyes of his. No, she decided. It was because he couldn't see her. Couldn't spot the way her pulse quickened whenever he was close or the way her lips burned, requiring that she moisten them repeatedly, for the taste of his.

She sighed. Would she never get past this ridiculous physical attraction that should have vanished eons ago?

"I know what she means," he said, his deep voice low and somehow soothing in the darkness. "I've been single for going on eight years and the loneliness creeps up on me sometimes."

"What do you mean?" She stared at him, wished she could see his eyes just now. "You have your son. How can you be lonely?" God knew, he'd probably had his pick of the single ladies in the county. Maybe even a few who weren't single. Anger stirred deep in her chest.

"Shared custody, remember?" He leaned his head back against the seat. "He came to my house on Friday, stayed until today. Now he's at her house until this Friday. It's a really crappy way to raise a kid. I hate it more than you can imagine."

Audrey didn't want to hear about his issues with *her*. Before she realized what she was doing, she'd crossed her arms over her chest and stared straight ahead. Couldn't help herself. Talking about the other woman—no matter that it was eighteen years later—made her angry still. Hurt, still. Maybe that hurt was the kind one never recovered from.

"I know I've said this a thousand times." His voice was soft now, gentle. "But I'm sorry for what I did. I love my son and I can't regret him, but I would give anything on this earth if I hadn't hurt you."

She moistened her dry lips for the hundredth time, worked hard to keep the anger and resentment out of her voice. "That was a long time ago, Colt."

"No amount of time will change how much I regret being so stupid."

Audrey had to bite her tongue to prevent saying she was glad to hear it. "We've all made mistakes."

He exhaled a big breath. "Some of us just make bigger ones than others."

"You think Sauder is in there?" She had to change the subject before she said something she would regret.

"I don't know, but if he is, I want to be here when he comes out."

Audrey didn't say anything else after that and neither did Colt. She considered powering down the window to let in some air. His aftershave was nicely understated, barely there in fact, but the soft scent of lemons and leather was driving her mad.

Maybe she should just close her eyes and pretend she was somewhere else.

Somewhere far away from Colt Tanner and the past that appeared determined to linger in the present.

Chapter Nine

Wednesday, February 27, 6:15 a.m.

Audrey woke to the gentle sound of rain, the lingering taste of chocolate in her mouth and the scent of Colt Tanner warming her senses. Would she never stop dreaming of the man?

"Morning."

She froze.

Car. Stakeout. Zimmerman place.

Her head was lying on his shoulder.

Audrey jerked upright. Banged her head on the seat back. "Good morning." She grabbed her bottle of water and busied herself with guzzling the remainder. Then she leaned forward and peered at the old farmhouse on the opposite side of the road. "Anything moving over there this morning?"

It was raining. Not hard, just drizzling, but enough to prevent opening a window.

"Couple of cows and a few chickens moving about."

She shot him a sour look. He grinned. "You know what I mean."

"No one has gone in or out the front door. No movement around the house, aside from what I've already told you about." That lopsided grin appeared again.

She glanced away, couldn't bear to look at him or see that grin. Not like this. "Should we knock on the door and ask him if he's seen his buddy Sauder?"

"How about pulling into the driveway? Then we'll go from there."

Audrey started the car, anticipation of something other than the man seated far too close to her zinging through her veins. She wanted the story on Sauder. This was big and it was happening right in her backyard. She parked behind Zimmerman's truck and shut off the engine.

"So let's see who's home." She reached for the door.

"*We* aren't going to see who's home, but I am." He opened the passenger-side door. "Stay put, Rey. I mean it."

"Whatever you say, Sheriff." She propped her arms on the steering wheel and stared straight ahead. It was easier to lie to him when she wasn't looking at him.

"Do not get out of this car," he reiterated before closing the door.

Mad as hell, she watched him climb the steps and cross the porch. Even more maddening was the idea that he still looked great after sleeping all night in a compact car. His shirt wasn't even wrinkled, but it was getting all wet in the rain, plastering to his body.

"You are so bad, Rey," she muttered as she glanced at her reflection in the rearview mirror. She groaned. Mascara was smudged beneath her eyes. Her hair was mussed.

From the corner of her eye she saw movement. A figure—a man—was running across the field beyond the house. She glanced at the front door. Zimmerman was talking to Colt.

Audrey bolted from the car and lunged across the yard, rain slapping her in the face. "He's running!"

Before she reached the fence, Colt darted ahead of her, flying over the fence with only one hand braced on the top rail to launch his body. The fleeing man was disappearing in the distance. She couldn't be certain it was Sauder, but who else would be running? Seemed like a very good question to ask the homeowner.

Audrey turned around and headed back to the house. Mr. Zimmerman stood on the porch watching the show. "Is that Wesley Sauder?"

Zimmerman shrugged. "Could be."

Which meant yes. "Mr. Zimmerman, you do realize…"

Before she could finish her statement, the man had turned and walked back into his house, closing the door behind him.

So much for neighborliness.

Audrey crossed the yard, then dropped back into the car and backed out of the driveway. She might as well drive in the direction Colt had disappeared. Whether he caught the guy or not he would need his cell phone, which was lying on the console, and he certainly would need a ride.

ABOUT A MILE beyond the Zimmerman driveway, Colt waited on the side of the road. The thick woods behind him were likely the reason he'd lost the running man. He was soaked to the bone, every inch of fabric clinging to his muscular body. Another groan emanated from her. She needed to take care of those basic needs or she was going to screw up royally.

Colt climbed into the passenger seat. "Lost him in the woods."

"I asked Zimmerman if that was Sauder and all he said was, 'Could be.' Then he went into the house and closed the door. I don't think he's going to be amenable to answering questions."

"At least we know Sauder is staying close."

They drove back to the Zimmerman house and Colt knocked on the door. No answer.

When Colt dropped back into the passenger seat, Audrey asked, "You really think that was him?" She headed back into town, doing everything within her power not to look at the way his wet clothes had molded to every square inch of him.

"I'm reasonably sure it was him all right. I got a pretty good look at him twice. I can't believe he outran me."

"I can't imagine it's easy to run in cowboy boots." She glanced down his long damp legs at the footwear in question.

"I guess I'm used to doing whatever I do in boots."

A vision of Colt kissing her senseless before pulling her into his truck filled her head. She blinked the memories away. Yes, he rarely pulled off his boots. But then they'd always taken the fastest route possible to what they wanted. She pushed away the thought. Reminded herself that she shouldn't be going there, particularly with him so close…so wet…and so…

Stop. Stop. Stop.

"If you'll drop me off at the paper, I'll get my truck and run to the house for a shower."

She cleared her throat, focused on the practical. "I need to do the same."

The silence that thickened between them for the rest of the drive had her reliving the time they had gotten caught in the rain, ending up soaked to the bones just as they were now. Only that time they had made love. Hard as she tried she could not make the images go away.

What in the world was she doing?

BY THAT AFTERNOON she and Brian had laid out a good, meaty article about organized crime and its reach for Thursday's edition of the *Gazette*. Somehow she had to find a way to get Sarah to talk to her. Maybe she should pay a visit to Nikki Slater again. If her husband was in trouble, would Sarah share her concerns with her best friend? Seemed the logical thing to do. Unless she was afraid of putting her friend in the crosshairs. Both Colt and Branch had warned that more of the men looking for Sauder—if that's what they were doing, and it appeared to be—would be coming. If Sauder had something they wanted or knew something he shouldn't, they wouldn't stop coming until they had handled the situation.

But what could this seemingly community-and family-oriented Mennonite man know about organized crime? He'd been living in Winchester for more than ten years.

Maybe it wasn't what he knew now, but something he had known before?

Audrey still had a few contacts in Chicago. She might as well reach out and rattle that cage, see what shook loose. Judd Seymour was the top crime beat reporter in the Windy City. Audrey called, got his voice mail and left him a message.

Brian poked his head into her office. "You have a minute?"

She smiled. "Always." She cringed as he sat down. "Oh, I forgot to put gas in your car and Colt got the passenger seat wet and the floorboard muddy. I'll pay for the cleaning."

Now that she thought about it, she'd been almost as wet and muddy as Colt. If she hadn't been so distracted by him in his wet clothes and the fact that Sauder had given them the slip, she might have taken better care of Brian's car.

Brian laughed. "Not to worry. I topped the tank off at lunch and dropped the car off for detailing at the car wash. You'll find a charge on the newspaper's account for all of the above."

"Good." She folded her arms over her chest and eyed her friend and partner in most crimes. "So, you set me up last evening."

Brian blushed. "Possibly. For the most part I was worried about you. I like having you here. I don't want to lose you."

"Mm-hmm."

"I really was," he argued. "Ezra Zimmerman lives in a pretty remote area. Besides, if you and

Colt can figure out the most likely places Sauder would hide, what makes you think the bad guys looking for him aren't able to do the same thing?"

Audrey laughed. "Okay, okay. All is forgiven."

He narrowed his gaze. "So, how did it go? I mean, you did spend the entire night in a rather cramped space with *him*."

"It was…fine." She nodded. "For the first time in eighteen years we didn't bite each other's heads off."

"Sounds like progress."

Before she could set him straight, her cell shuddered against her desk. "Excuse me." She grabbed her phone.

Brian stood. "Back to the grind."

She gave him a salute and answered the call. "Audrey Anderson."

"Audrey, how are you?"

Judd Seymour.

"Judd, hey, thanks for returning my call." After her exit from the *Post*, she was surprised he even bothered. Unless, of course, he'd heard about the shootings. She was more than happy to juggle a little quid pro quo.

"Anytime, Audrey. You will always be my favorite Southern lady."

Oh yeah. He wanted information. "Good to hear, Judd. What can you tell me about the organized crime in your fair city?"

"It just so happens that I've been doing a little research on the Cicero family."

"Perfect. The Cicero family is the one I'm primarily interested in."

"They've been around for a very long time, Audrey. Five generations."

"Yeah, I read that online. I also read that the current head of the family has a trial coming up. The Feds have been putting the evidence together for years, trying to get this guy on a docket. You think the trial has anything to do with what's going on in my little town?" Didn't seem possible, but stranger things had happened.

"As far-fetched as it sounds, I think that's a strong likelihood."

"I need more than your conclusions, Judd. What makes you believe this is the case?"

"I did a little digging," he went on. "Twenty-odd years ago, Winchester showed up in an investigation on the old man, Louis Cicero. Nothing came of it, but I thought it was strange that Winchester, Tennessee, a speck on the map, would be mentioned in the pile of documents related to all the crimes the cops and the Feds can't seem to prove against the family. To tell you the truth, I don't think they'll ever get this trial started. They have some circumstantial evidence, but they just don't have anything solid enough and no witnesses."

A rush of cold poured through her. "Was there a person's name mentioned in connection with Winchester?"

The sound of papers shifting went on for a few seconds. "No name, just that there was a snippet of discussion picked up on the wiretaps. Winchester was mentioned several times. It reads like the old man thought there was trouble of some sort down there. But no names. Criminals tend to use code words, you know. Sometimes the Feds figure them out, sometimes they don't. They've always needed someone on the inside of the organization, but no one who dares talk about the Cicero family ever lives long enough to do it in front of a camera or a judge."

"You said twenty-odd years ago. Exactly when was this?" A choking sensation made it difficult for Audrey to breathe.

"Let's see. The notes show that the first mention was just before Christmas more than twenty-four years ago. The final mention was March 15 the following year."

"What was said about March 15?" Her voice sounded stilted, felt raw. March 15, twenty-four years ago, her father had his heart attack and died...and the thing in the basement happened.

More shuffling of pages. "Here we go. The transcript says, 'We've lost interest in Winchester.'"

"Whatever they thought would happen or was

happening fell apart, I guess," she suggested. Or died. Her heart was beating so fast she could hardly breathe.

"Based on what I'm reading, I'd say there was something or someone in Winchester they wanted but it didn't work out."

"Thank you, Judd." She forced a laugh. "I'm not sure what any of that means, but now I know the connection."

"Two of the Cicero family's people have managed to get themselves dead in your town, Audrey. What's going on down there?"

"I wish I knew, Judd. I really do." She shared what she could. Basically what the paper had printed so far. She owed it to Colt to keep quiet about what happened at the Zimmerman place this morning.

"Keep me posted, will you?"

"Sure thing. I hope you'll do the same."

"I will. Good to hear from you, Audrey."

When the call ended, Audrey pulled up her contacts and tapped another number. Since her mother's memories were lost, there was only one other person she could ask about twenty-four years ago.

PHILLIP ANDERSON WAS only too happy to drop by the newspaper after his racquetball game. He played every Wednesday afternoon. He was dressed in sweats when he arrived. Audrey took his wet umbrella and propped it in the corner. It had been raining off and on all day. The same was forecast for tonight. It was that time of year. She rounded up a bottle of water for Phil and closed the door to her office.

Phillip frowned. "Has something happened to Mary Jo?"

"Oh, sorry. No. Mom's okay." She shrugged. "No change."

He nodded and took a long swallow of water. Phillip was five years younger than his only sibling, his brother—her father, who had died twenty-four years ago next month. He was sixty-two; her father would be sixty-seven if he were still alive.

"When Dad was still alive, did he or the newspaper ever have any trouble with organized crime?"

Phillip coughed, almost choked. "What?"

"Was there any trouble that you were aware of between Dad and a representative of organized crime from, say, Chicago?"

Phillip sat his bottle of water aside and sat up a little straighter. "What's this about, Rey?"

"During the four or five months before Dad died, there was something going on with one of the organized crime elements in Chicago and there were comments about Winchester. My source believes there was something here they wanted."

"If something like that was going on," he said,

"we sure as hell didn't know about it, because it would have been on the front page if we had. You know your father was one to push the envelope. He wouldn't have sat on something like that."

She did know that. But she also knew her father had died suddenly and that a stranger had been in his office at the time. "Do you remember anyone from out of town who visited the office during that time?"

More frown lines formed on his face. Phillip and her father had looked very much alike as younger men. She imagined this was what her dad would look like now. Lots of laugh lines with that deep, booming voice that resonated through a crowd. Everyone had liked her dad.

Her heart hurt at the idea that he'd died so young. Only a few years older than she was now.

"I can't say that I do, but you know Porter was always searching for ways to expand and to increase circulation. He had more visitors than a head of state. I was like Brian, more focused on editorial and production. Your father was the businessman. The face of the *Gazette*."

Hearing her uncle talk about her dad had memories of him echoing inside her. The sound of his voice, the breadth of his strong shoulders and the smile that always told her everything was all right. As much as she missed him, she could only imagine how much her mother did. He had been her everything. After he died, she threw herself into raising Audrey and taking care of things around their big old house. And of course there were her civic duties. Mary Jo Anderson lived to support community fund-raisers. But there was always a sadness about her.

Still was.

"You're not thinking your father had some affiliation with criminal activity?"

His indignant tone said all that needed to be said on the matter.

"Of course not," she assured him. "On the contrary, I'm worried he may have known something that garnered the wrong attention, which is why I asked about visitors during that time frame."

Phillip nodded. "I'll study on it. If I think of anything or anyone, I'll be sure to let you know."

"Thank you, Phillip."

"We still on for dinner on Sunday?"

He and her mother had shared Sunday dinner for as long as she could remember. When she was a child, her father was there, too, of course. As was Phillip's wife. But she was gone now, too.

How long would it be before no one was left except Audrey?

But right now she still had her mom and uncle. "I look forward to it."

Audrey walked him out. He bragged about how he'd beaten the mayor again this afternoon. Two weeks in a row now. When he'd gone, she wandered back into the building. She had the sudden, nearly overwhelming urge to visit her mom. Talking about her dad always made her yearn to hug her mom.

Frantic voices and crying whispered through her mind. The two of them shared a bond that no one else could ever be a part of. Not even Phillip. There were some things that had to stay in the past. No matter what happened.

Audrey paused at the bottom of the stairs. Instead of going back up to her office, she went around behind the staircase and opened the door to the basement. She never went down there. Never.

But there came a time when a person had to face her fears. Face the part of her past that haunted her. Considering what Judd Seymour had told her and what was happening with Wesley Sauder, today was that day for Audrey. She couldn't keep pretending that what was down there had nothing to do with what was happening. Because somehow it did. No matter that twenty-four years had passed, there was a connection, perhaps a thin one but a connection nonetheless.

She opened the door and flipped the light switch. Fluorescent lights blinked and buzzed until the artificial glare filled the darkness. She took the three steps across the landing and began the descent down the iron staircase that reminded her of the fire escape on the outside of the building. Both of the interior staircases, this one as well as the one leading to the second floor, were made of iron and offered a very urban, industrial feel. The interior of the first and second floors had been redone in the fifties and then again in the nineties. Before long Audrey would need to put her stamp on things. For now, she couldn't imagine changing a thing.

If only she could make this part go away.

There was nothing particularly eerie about the basement. The walls were brick, as was the rest of the building. Shelves lined the walls. On the shelves were boxes and plastic containers filled with ancient memorabilia as well as all the things that two hundred years of living collected. There was a musty smell in the air. The dampness Brian told her about, she acknowledged. Somehow water was seeping from beneath the concrete. Portions of the floor looked wet. Brian was right in that the issue needed to be addressed at some point. She just had to figure out a way to do it without anyone learning her and her mother's secret.

The basement floor had once been brick, but plumbing renovations when she was twelve had required that a large portion be dug up. Once the work was complete, her mother had ordered concrete poured over the entire floor. To level it and make it more stable, she'd insisted.

They had thought that would be the end of it.

Audrey walked to the center of the room and stared at the floor. "Who were you and what the hell did you want?"

Chapter Ten

With most of his deputies searching the county for Wesley Sauder and that crucial forty-eight-hour mark in the investigation rapidly approaching, Colt was just about at his wit's end with Sarah. He stopped by her daddy's place again, but Aaron told him she'd gone back home since her house had been released. Sarah's kids had gathered around their uncle and stared expectantly at Colt as if he had the answer to what was going on in their suddenly upside-down lives.

More than a little frustrated, he had then gone to the Sauder home and gotten no answer after knocking repeatedly. Pulling into the bakery parking lot he now understood why. Sarah's minivan was there. The open sign on the door was flashing. His evidence techs were loading into their van—the one that had cost the county an arm and a leg. The rain had let up for a bit. Nothing like conducting a search in the rain.

The driver, Deputy Roland England, powered

his window down as Colt approached. "I was just about to call you, Sheriff."

"Did you finish your second sweep?" His rule was that every crime scene received at least two sweeps by his evidence techs. Almost every time, something new was found the second time around.

"We collected a good deal of trace evidence, but who knows if it's anything relevant. By the way, we were packing up when Branch dropped by. He said he'd need to see whatever we found since the Marshals were taking over the case. He was supposed to call you about it."

He had called and Colt hadn't answered. He shook his head, set his hands on his hips. "Is Sarah in there?"

"She just got here." England glanced at his new partner, Jonathan Gates. "We heard Branch talking on the phone. Sounds like they're pretty sure Wesley is some kind of federal fugitive."

Damn it. So they had info they weren't sharing. Irritation coiled in Colt's gut. He glanced around, didn't see Branch's truck. "Is he still in there?"

"After that call he had to leave, said he'd be right back."

His absence gave Colt a little time, maybe not much, but something. He nodded to his deputies. "All right then. Let me know what the lab says as soon as you can."

"Yes, sir."

As the van rolled out of the parking lot, Colt strode to the door of the bakery. The curtain in the window moved. Probably Sarah. He hoped she would be more cooperative today. This might be her last opportunity to talk to him.

The bell jingled as he opened the door. Sarah glanced up from behind the counter as if she hadn't known he was outside and pushed a smile into place. The expression didn't reach her eyes. Frankly, she didn't have a thing to be smiling about. Her husband and her father were at odds. And now her husband was hiding from serious trouble. Not to mention her husband's past had caused her to have to kill at least one man. And another man had been shot and killed in her place of business. In Colt's opinion, she had her hands full.

He glanced around, didn't see any sign of a co-worker. "Afternoon, Sarah."

She gave a nod. "Sheriff. I just pulled fresh muffins out of the oven."

He might not have much time, so he should get right to the point. "Sarah." He removed his hat and stood face-to-face with her, only the counter separating them. "I know you're worried and scared, and you have every right to be."

"Sheriff, I've already told you and Marshal Hol-

loway all I know. Wesley left home to attend a funeral and I haven't seen him since."

"He was at Ezra Zimmerman's place last night.
I'm guessing another friend in the community is
hiding him today."

She looked away, busied herself with placing a
row of freshly baked muffins from the pan into
the glass display case.

"I don't know enough about whatever life he's
running from to say whether your husband was
a bad man or not—"

"He's a good man," she snapped. "Everyone
knows that. Wesley has never caused any trouble
here. He has a long-standing reputation of helping
folks. You know that, Sheriff. So does everyone
else around here."

Until now, Colt didn't mention, and the man
suddenly appeared hell-bent on making up for
lost time and then some. "I know that, Sarah. I'm
not accusing Wesley of anything bad. But the
Marshals aren't looking at this the way I am. I'm
looking at Wesley as the husband and father—the
farmer and the pillar of the community—I know
him to be. But I'm the only member of law enforcement who's doing that. No offense to Branch,
but he doesn't know Wesley. This is strictly about
the case for him. Unless you tell me how to find
Wesley first, I can't help him."

Her watery eyes lifted to meet his. "You promise you'll protect him?"

"You have my word that I will protect him or die trying."

"He's a good man, Sheriff. He's not that person anymore...the one those horrible men are hunting. He had no idea they were coming for him when they showed up here. The one you found in the stockroom surprised him. He had a gun. Wesley had no choice; he had to defend himself. At the same time that other man was breaking into our home. He was going to use me and the kids to make Wesley do what he wanted. We both did what we had to do."

"Do you know why they're after Wesley?"

She shook her head. "He said the less I knew the safer I was. I haven't seen him since that night, Sheriff. I swear. He's hiding and I don't blame him. They want him dead. He knows things they don't want to come out. That's all I know. They'll do anything to stop him. Wesley begged me to take the children and hide, but I can't do that. We need this business to be operating if we're to survive. My kids are safe with my brother."

"I'll have a deputy watching after you, Sarah. But tell me, where would Wesley go?" Even as he asked the question he heard a vehicle arrive. He glanced over his shoulder, spotted Branch's truck parked next to his. "Tell me where to look. I will find him and I will protect him through this."

"Try James Ed Wenger. He and Wesley are friends."

The bell jingled, announcing Branch's arrival.

"I'll take one of those fresh muffins," Colt said. "If the coffee's fresh, I'll have some of that, too."

"Hey, Colt." Branch joined him at the counter as Sarah busied herself filling his order. "I left you a voice mail. We need to talk."

"I was just about to call you back." Colt gave him a nod. "My evidence techs were still here when I arrived. I understand you have an update for me."

Branch hitched his head toward the door. "Let's talk outside."

Colt tapped the counter. "Be right back, Sarah."

The door jingled and they waited for a woman, a child on each hip, to come in before exiting. Branch walked over to his truck and opened the driver's-side door. Colt waited near the hood. He understood jurisdiction and all that legal stuff, but this was his county. He had been elected to serve and protect the people within its boundaries. As much as he appreciated help from the TBI fellows, the FBI and the Marshals occasionally, he didn't appreciate having an investigation taken over by anyone else.

Branch placed a manila file on the hood and

opened it. "This is Thomas Bateman." He tapped the photo that was obviously a younger Wesley Sauder.

"All right." Colt moved a little closer so he could see the next photo or page in Branch's show-and-tell.

"This—" he tapped another photo, this one of an older man "—is Louis Cicero. He's the current boss of the Cicero family. His father was the patriarch before him and so on. They're one of the oldest organized crime families in the country. Various members of the family have been prosecuted for all manner of illegal activities over the years, but we've never been able to make the big charges stick and we sure as hell have never been able to nail one of the top guys." He flipped back to the photo of Bateman, aka Wesley Sauder. "But this guy could nail Louis Cicero. Cicero has one son—Louis Jr. They call him L.J. He and Bateman were best friends. Bateman worked with *the* accountant who took care of Cicero business. Bateman was being groomed to take over one day when he cut and run. Rumor is, he took a serious piece of evidence with him."

"How the hell did he end up a Mennonite?" Talk about going undercover. Then again, with the mob after him, he had to be desperate for a deep cover.

Branch shrugged. "We can't be sure how that

happened. I assume he happened upon this Wesley Sauder—who died around that same time—and decided to claim his identity. It happens all the time. An accountant would certainly know how to make that happen. He was able to vanish just like that." Branch snapped his fingers. "He'd probably been planning his escape for a while. He was sitting pretty and making big money when he jumped ship."

"So he was part of this mob family?" Damn. Colt felt bad for Sarah. She would be devastated.

"In a white-collar way," Branch explained. "We have no reason to believe he ever killed anyone. But he was involved, yes."

"So what prompted his change of heart? He had to know they would come looking for him."

"He was in love with Louis's daughter, Sophia, but her father wanted her to marry a man in another crime family, an effort to mesh the two families. When her father wouldn't be dissuaded, Sophia realized her only way out was to go to the FBI and try to help take her father down. Bateman agreed to do this with her. She ended up dead and he disappeared."

A new tension trickled through Colt. "Did he have anything to do with her death?"

"Chicago PD investigated and concluded that she was killed by a crazed crackhead. She was a victim of circumstance—in the wrong place at the wrong time, according to their report. Said crackhead ended up dead in his cell. Hanged himself with his pants."

"Bateman lost it and decided he had to get away?" Didn't make a whole lot of sense for a guy sitting pretty, as Branch put it, in a mob family. Bateman hadn't gotten where he was at the time by being stupid. He lost the woman he loved, but why throw everything else away? Even Colt knew that a man just didn't leave an organized crime family once he was in—particularly as deep as Bateman had been.

"Sophia was young and idealistic," Branch explained. "Her father's intentions for her made it easy for her to decide to go after him. She wanted out of the family business and she was willing to sell Daddy out to make it happen. Despite the seemingly cut-and-dry circumstances of her death, the FBI believes her father discovered what she was up to and ordered her executed."

God Almighty. "Do you think her own father had her killed?"

Branch nodded. "I do. So does everyone else who worked the federal side of the investigation. At any rate, she and Bateman hadn't turned over what the agent needed to move on Cicero. At the time, the thinking was that after she was murdered Bateman took the evidence as a sort of insurance for his future."

"Does Sarah know about this Sophia Cicero?" Colt could just imagine how she would feel knowing her husband had lived this sort of life before showing up here. But to know he did so because he'd loved another woman would be a hard pill to swallow. Worse, Sarah had to feel as if their marriage and their children were nothing more than a cover for him to stay hidden from the reach of his former life. Yet she wanted to protect him. She loved him despite it all, that was clear.

"If she does, she's not talking." Branch shook his head. "We need her to cooperate."

Colt scrubbed a hand over his jaw. "Bateman is a possible witness in a major federal case. I guess I can see why you need to assume control of the investigation."

"It's not personal, Colt," Branch assured him. "We have an opportunity here and we have to be extremely careful. Cicero has murdered dozens of people, not to mention he's thought to be supplying drugs and guns at an unparalleled level and pace. We need to stop him and his organization once and for all. Bateman—Sauder—can make that happen."

Colt nodded. "I'll do everything in my power to help."

Branch clapped him on the back. "We appreciate it. Your deputies need to be on their toes. Cicero will keep sending his people until he finds

Bateman. You can count on that. They won't think twice about killing anyone who gets in their way."

Colt got it. No one was safe until Bateman was found.

Sarah met him at the bakery door with his bag of goodies. Her eyes told him all he needed to know. She was counting on him to protect her husband…to protect her future.

With his coffee ensconced in the cup holder and his muffin in hand, Colt headed for the office. His first step was to get the word out to his deputies that he needed everyone focused 24/7 on finding Sauder until this was done. Next, he intended to talk to Audrey about letting folks in the community know they had to take the necessary precautions. A press conference couldn't be put off any longer.

AFTER BRIEFING HIS deputies and arranging a press conference for five that evening, Colt dropped by the paper. He wanted to give Rey a heads-up. He'd promised her an exclusive and he intended to deliver on that promise. She would want to be at the press conference. He'd told his assistant he would notify the *Gazette* personally.

As soon as he walked into the lobby he spotted Rey in her office. He removed his hat and stood for a moment staring up at her beyond the glass wall. Each of the offices had a glass wall that looked out over the lobby. She was arranging something on the small conference table in her office. Maybe the layout for tomorrow's paper.

He liked watching her. The way she moved, so purposeful yet so graceful, the way her blond hair fell around her shoulders. Most of all he loved to hear her talk. Loved her laugh. Mostly, he loved everything about her. She was the most beautiful woman he had ever laid eyes on. No matter the hurt that stood between them and the years that had passed; he still considered her his.

Not smart, Colt.

"Good afternoon, Sheriff. May I help you?"

He drew his gaze from Rey to the receptionist. "Morning, Tanya. I was just going up to see Rey."

"Sure. I'll let her know you're on the way up."

He crossed the room and climbed the iron staircase. Rey's father had been into transparency before it became a popular buzzword. The offices had their glass walls, and so did the printing room and the big conference room. The local schoolkids loved touring the building and seeing the way the news business worked. Visitors and clients could see the inner workings firsthand by just walking into the lobby. No matter that Rey had traveled the world and had such an exciting career; he had always believed this was where she belonged.

She waited for him at her office door. "I'm hoping your visit is about news on the case. I have a big hole in tomorrow's front page."

"I have plenty to share, you just can't print all of it yet."

She gave a nod. "Come in. Let's hear what you've got."

Colt spent the next twenty minutes explaining everything Branch had told him. Rey listened, nodded occasionally, but didn't ask any questions. He was beginning to think Branch had already spoken to her when she finally reacted.

"You want to warn the community to be on the lookout for any suspicious strangers."

This wasn't a question. She understood that he had a responsibility to do just that. "To the best of my ability. I can't mention the Cicero family, I can only tell them to report any suspicious activity or strangers who approach them asking questions about any other residents."

"Wow." She leaned back in her chair. "You live in a small town to avoid this kind of thing and then it comes to you."

"Someone usually brings it," he pointed out.

She nodded but she seemed preoccupied. She had appeared to be distracted the whole time he was bringing her up to speed. Something wasn't right. "You okay, Rey? I mean, you seem particularly unsettled by all this."

"Do you remember when we were kids, your

father ever talking about anything like this? You know, organized crime in Franklin County?"

He thought about her question for a moment, then shook his head. "There's been the occasional locally organized crime. A drug lab. We even had a team of counterfeiters once. But nothing like this, that crossed state lines."

"I just remember overhearing some things my dad said when I was about twelve. I've checked the files, there weren't any particular stories about organized crime going on at the time, certainly nothing beyond our state lines. But there was something. I just haven't found it yet. A contact of mine in Chicago said there were mentions of Winchester in some of the wiretaps the Feds had done on one or the other crime families in Chicago."

That was news to Colt. "Branch didn't mention anything, but I'll ask him."

She nodded. "I appreciate it. So, I'll put together what I can for tomorrow's paper and urge the folks to be on the lookout."

Colt took that as his cue and stood. "I'll be on my way." He settled his hat into place. "Just so you know, I enjoyed having your company during last night's stakeout."

She blushed and that made him smile. "As I recall, you hijacked *my* stakeout."

He grinned. "I guess I did."

He was at her door when he worked up the nerve to ask the other question on his mind. He turned back to her. "Maybe we can talk about the case some more over dinner?"

She smiled. "Maybe."

He gave her a nod and went on his way. It wasn't a yes, but it wasn't the usual hell no, either.

They were making progress.

Chapter Eleven

Franklin County Veterinary Clinic

Audrey waved to Burt Johnston's receptionist as she passed through the lobby. Burt had told her to come on back at quarter to four. The yapping of dogs accompanied her trek toward the offices. This was the largest clinic in the county. Burt took care of everything from birds to horses. He didn't really do much of the hands-on work himself anymore. There were four veterinarians and several assistants. He mostly oversaw the operation and focused on being the county coroner.

She waved to one of the techs she'd gone to high school with before knocking on Burt's closed door. The other woman was busy examining a black Lab. Audrey hadn't had a dog or a cat since she was a kid. Now that she was back home maybe she should think about getting one.

The big old house was a lot lonelier than she

remembered. Of course she'd never lived there alone before. A dog would be nice.

"Audrey, if that's you, come on in. If it's anyone else, go away."

She laughed as she opened the door. "It's me."

He dropped his feet from his desk to the floor and sat up straight. "Close the door behind you." He closed the romance novel he was reading and tucked it into a drawer.

Audrey did as he asked and moved a cat from the chair in front of his desk. The animal curled around her ankle and purred. "Good kitty." She lowered into the chair and stroked the furry beast now stretching and rolling on the floor. She did all this so Burt wouldn't see her grinning about his secret attraction to romance novels. Her mother had told her when she was a kid that Burt loved to read the same books she did. She made Audrey promise not to tell and she never had.

He finished off his cola and sat the can on his desk. "You want chocolate?" He held the bag of chocolate candy up for her to see.

"No thanks."

He stuffed another piece into his mouth before hiding the bag in the file cabinet behind his desk. "Ever since the heart attack I have to hide everything I enjoy."

"Mrs. Johnston wants to take care of you." A

wiry tail switched back and forth as the cat waited for more attention. Audrey scratched at her belly.

"There are some things a man needs and, for me, those things are my chocolate, my books and the occasional nip of bourbon." He shrugged. "The way I see it, what she doesn't know won't hurt her."

Audrey understood now. "Your staff would tell her about the chocolate if they knew." She nodded toward the file cabinet.

"Spies," he griped. "Every one of them."

She bit back the smile. "I'm certain they mean well."

He grunted. "So how can I help you today, Audrey? You want to know something about those two bodies?"

"Actually, I wanted to talk to you about my dad."

His bushy eyebrows knit together as his face furrowed into a frown. "That was a while ago, Rey. He had a heart attack. There wasn't any need for an autopsy. His personal physician confirmed a diagnosis of coronary artery disease. He was young for the disease to have been so advanced, but that's the way it is sometimes. He'd been taking medicine, but sometimes it's just too little, too late. Your momma witnessed the heart attack so there wasn't any question about cause of death. What specifically about his death is on your mind?"

"Did you examine his body closely? The way you would one when foul play is suspected?" She doubted he did but she needed to know.

"Now that I did. In those days I was still learning a lot. Much of taking care of animals is the same as taking care of humans, but there are still considerable differences. Every new body was an opportunity to familiarize myself with procedure. To tell you the truth, every body tells a different story. Edward DuPont taught me a lot. He says you can read a body the same way you can a book. His daughter says the same thing. She spoke of it in that book she wrote, *The Language of Death*."

Rowan DuPont was older than Audrey but she remembered her. She'd had a twin sister who drowned. Not long after her mother had hanged herself. Tragic. The DuPonts always seemed a little strange. Maybe it was because they lived and worked in the family funeral home.

Audrey shifted her thoughts back to her father. "Did you note any signs of a struggle? Bruises or scratches?"

Burt opened his mouth, but then snapped it shut. "Give me a minute. Do you have time for me to pull the file?"

Audrey moistened her lips and nodded. "Absolutely."

He turned his back to her and started riffling through the drawers of the file cabinets lining the wall behind his desk. "The clinic's files are in the file room. These files are related to my work as coroner."

"How long have you been serving as coroner?" She couldn't remember but she knew he was in the position when her father died. Seeing his face and hearing his reassuring words had stuck with her all these years. There wasn't a lot about that night she remembered, but Burt was one part she did recall.

"Here we go." He shoved the drawer closed and turned to settle back into his chair.

Audrey reminded herself to breathe.

Burt placed the manila folder on his desk. It looked so innocuous. Like hundreds of others in this building and back at her office at the newspaper. But this one was very different. Inside that folder were the final reports related to her father's last moments of life and his death.

Burt glanced up at her. "You're welcome to look at the file yourself, if you'd like."

She held up a hand and shook her head. She wasn't sure she could bear to see the photos. "You can give it to me in layman's terms."

"All right. So there was a small scratch on the side of his neck. Nothing significant. He could have done it shaving that morning or even scratching himself." Burt made humming sounds as he perused the file. The sort that suggested he was questioning what he was reading or was confused by it somehow.

Her nerves were jangling by the time he looked up over his glasses. "There was a bruise on his right shoulder. One on his lower back. And another on his left shin. My notes show that your mother said he'd taken a tumble down the stairs the night before."

"Oh." Audrey nodded. "I remember now." This was a lie, but she understood that if her mother had told that story, it needed to be told.

Burt studied her for a long moment. "Is there something you're worried about related to your father's death?"

The words were on her tongue. But she couldn't share her true concerns with him or anyone else. "No. No. It's something one of my contacts said to me about this Sauder case."

Burt closed the file and cocked his head. "I am now thoroughly confused."

"He has evidence that during the same time frame, when my dad died, there was some organized crime activity related to the same group involved in the Sauder case going on in Winchester. He couldn't say what the connection was, just that it involved Winchester at that particular time. Colt said he doesn't recall anything happening at that time but he's going to check his files."

Burt tapped his forefinger against his chin.

"There was a little something-something going on at the newspaper. Mary Jo should remember. As I recall Porter said there was a push coming from up north to buy up a bunch of newspapers around here, in Alabama and Georgia. You know, Southern small-town papers. I don't recall the reasoning, but Phil said Porter was fired up about it. That was perhaps a month before he passed."

Audrey's heart pounded a little harder with each word he uttered. "Did my father mention anyone calling him or visiting him in relationship to this push to buy?"

"No, not that I remember. You should ask Phil. I'm certain he would know. He and your father were partners after all."

But Phillip had said he knew nothing—that her dad knew nothing—about any issues related to organized crime. Had he been left out of the loop? Or had he lied to her? She couldn't exactly call him a liar. What she needed was some sort of evidence.

"Thanks, Burt, for looking into this for me." She stood and reached across his desk, offering her hand.

He pushed to his feet, gave her hand a shake. "You let me know if there's anything else I can assist you with. I'm always happy to try to help solve a good mystery."

All of these pieces of information definitely met the criteria for a mystery.

As Audrey left the clinic she couldn't stop obsessing on the idea that Phillip had lied to her. Her mom's story about the fall down the stairs was the only explanation she could have given to cover for the bruises.

How else was she going to explain what really happened without confessing to murder?

PINE HAVEN REALLY was a lovely place if one had to be imprisoned. In reality it was a prison of sorts. Or maybe the minds of the residents were the real prisons. Her mother was physically fit, but her mind had let her down. Now she had to live like *this*.

Audrey regretted the thought instantly. Facilities like Pine Haven were a godsend in situations like her mom's. Yet it felt wrong to keep her here. She had loved that big old rambling house. She would have stayed there until the day she died if not for her inability to remember what she'd done two minutes ago. Like walking out of the house and leaving the burner turned on under an empty teakettle. Or the faucet running in the tub. Or the door unlocked. The car running in the garage. All those things had happened and Audrey had been left with no choice.

She found her mom on the terrace staring out

over the beautifully landscaped grounds. Audrey sat down in the chair beside her. "It's a lovely day."

"It surely is," her mom said, not taking her eyes from whatever was in those trees that held her spellbound. Buds were opening, and soon the leaves would unfurl and fill the branches. The grass would need to be cut. Shrubs were already sprouting errant twigs. Tulips, daffodils, crocuses and hyacinths filled the mounds around trees and the urns strategically stationed around the terrace. Her mom loved flowers. The beauty of this place was one of the reasons Audrey had chosen it over several others. Plus it was close to home.

"I went to see Burt Johnston today."

Mary Jo turned to face her. "How is Burt?"

"He's well. His usual jovial self. Reading his romance novels and sneaking chocolate."

Mary Jo laughed. "He always did love those romance novels. And Iris? Is she keeping his sugar down? He gave her such fits about his diet. Poor woman has the patience of Job."

Audrey didn't bother reminding her mom that Iris would never be able to keep Burt Johnston on the straight and narrow where his chocolate was concerned. She wouldn't remember it five minutes from now. "He said Dad had bruises in several places on his body when he died."

Mary Jo nodded, her eyes still tracking Audrey's. "I told Burt he'd fallen down the stairs, but that wasn't true. You know it wasn't true." She looked back to the trees. "I don't even remember all the lies I had to tell in the days after he died. I could only do whatever necessary to keep you safe. To ensure no one ever knew what really happened."

Audrey's heart ached. "Did he fight with that man?"

Mary Jo's face pinched with confusion. "What man?"

"The man who tried to hurt Dad. Did he fight with him?"

"Oh my, I don't know." She shook her head. "You know we don't talk about that man. It's best never to speak of him again."

If only that were possible. "Mom, did Uncle Phillip know about the man?"

She looked properly horrified. "Why, heavens no." Then her face scrunched up again. "At least I don't think so. He wasn't there. You know, he was always gone somewhere when your father needed him most. Probably taking some girl out. He was a rascal back then, your uncle Phillip."

"You're certain Dad didn't tell him about the trouble from the man?"

"No, no, your father died. He couldn't tell anyone."

Audrey sighed. This was pointless. "I mean before he died. Did he tell Uncle Phillip before he died about the trouble with the man?"

She stared at Audrey for a long moment before asking, "What man?"

Audrey sat in silence with her mom for a long while. Then she hugged her and gave her a kiss goodbye. She doubted the secrets her mother kept from those days could ever be exhumed. Maybe she was right and Phillip knew nothing about whatever the man wanted and whoever had sent him.

But Audrey knew something. She knew in all likelihood that the man who had sent two killers—so far—to find Wesley Sauder was the same man who sent the one who tried to kill her dad.

She drove across town, turned into the parking lot of the newspaper and sat for a while staring at the building. She had a few minutes before the press conference Colt had scheduled. She couldn't remember very much about that night all those years ago. Her mind had blocked the most painful parts. She remembered her mother screaming. Audrey had been in her uncle Phillip's office. So Phillip hadn't been there. She couldn't have been playing in his office if he had been there. She remembered going round and round in the chair behind his desk. There was that strange pop, and then her mother was screaming.

Audrey remembered seeing the man on the floor...and all the blood.

Voices echoed in her head. Her mom's. Her dad's. The other man wasn't talking. He was down...on the floor.

Jack...her dad had called him Jack.

Audrey dug in her bag for her cell phone. She called Judd Seymour. "Hey, Judd, you have a minute?"

"I do but only one. I'm on my way to a meeting."

She could hear the city sounds in the background. Horns blowing. Cab drivers shouting. Those were the sounds that had once followed her to sleep at night and greeted her each morning. She did not miss the big city.

The admission startled her. It was the first time she'd felt that way, or at least the first time she'd recognized she felt that way since returning to Winchester. Was her new life here growing on her? Wasn't coming back home supposed to be temporary?

No time for that kind of soul-searching.

"During that time frame we talked about— twenty-four years ago—do you remember a guy connected to the organized crime family named Jack? You know, the family from the wiretaps?"

"Jack Torrino? Is that who you're referring to?"

The name didn't ring any bells for Audrey. "I can't be certain. I only have the name Jack."

"Torrino is the only Jack I'm familiar with from that era. He would have been affiliated with the same family we discussed before. Why do you ask?"

"I think maybe he was in Winchester in March of that year."

"Well, if that's the case, you've just solved a quarter-century-old mystery, because twenty-four years ago Jack Torrino disappeared. No one has a clue what happened to him or where he ended up."

"Thanks, Judd."

The call ended and Audrey sat very still. She knew exactly where Jack Torrino was.

Chapter Twelve

Colt climbed back into his truck and sat there for a long moment. The press conference had gone off without a hitch. Branch as well as Chief of Police Billy Brannigan had been on either side of him. Colt had warned the citizens of Franklin County to be on the lookout for any suspicious activities and to report any such activities or strangers to the hotlines his department had set up. Since the press conference he had interviewed several of Sauder's closest friends and not one owned up to having seen him. Sarah had told him he would have a difficult time getting any of them to speak against her husband. They all knew what Colt wanted: to find Sauder. Somehow they all managed to avoid giving him any information without actually lying. Even Wenger had played him off.

He was getting nowhere way too fast.

Colt started his truck and drove to the only other place he could think of where he might learn something. It was a long shot, but it was the only shot he had at this point. Wesley Sauder or Thomas Bateman, whoever he considered himself to be these days, was going to get himself dead otherwise.

The Cow Palace didn't open until nine but most of the staff would be there prepping for the coming night. Colt had frequented the place with a fake ID like most of his friends during his senior year. His own wild behavior that year was what scared him the most about his son. Colt knew the trouble he'd gotten into; he didn't want Key to go there. Colt had been a pretty good kid, but he'd had his moments. Any one of those moments could have turned out far worse and he could have lost his life.

It was bad enough that he'd lost Audrey.

His son wasn't speaking to him at the moment. Not a big surprise. He'd given Colt the silent treatment whenever he was angry since the divorce. Not that he could fault the boy. He'd learned the tactic from his mother. Colt was far from perfect and he'd made his share of mistakes with their son, but Karen was a user. He hoped like hell he could prevent Key from following that path. A man was only as good as his word. Failing to live up to it, just once, could turn out to be the biggest mistake of his life.

Colt thought of Rey. If he hadn't broken his word to her…

Too late to go there now. He had broken his word. The only good thing to come of that misstep was his son. Somehow he had to make sure he didn't screw up the most important thing in his life—being a father.

And one way or another he would find a way to win Rey's trust again. He didn't want to spend the next eighteen years without her in his life—completely.

THE COW PALACE sat between Winchester and Decherd. The building had once been a livestock market where horses and cattle—mostly the latter—were brought for sale to the highest bidder. His daddy had brought him to the auctions a few times when he was a kid. By the time he was fifteen, the market had moved to a different, larger location between Winchester and Fayetteville. The old building, which looked like a large barn, had sat empty for a couple of years. Then some enterprising group had come up with the bright idea to turn it into a saloon. The Cow Palace had been born.

Folks came from all over to attend the celebrity events held in the now-famous venue. The building had been expanded three times. After the divorce Colt had frequented the place for a time and then he'd realized he wasn't going to find what he was looking for there. He'd been divorced nearly eight years now and he hadn't found the right one yet.

Maybe that was a sign that he'd let the only right one for him get away when he was too young and dumb to realize the magnitude of his mistake.

He parked and strode across the parking lot. There was no changing the past. But maybe he could divert the course of Sarah Sauder's husband's future. Because if he didn't find him soon, his kids were going to grow up without a father. Branch Holloway had lived away far too long. Folks didn't know him the way they did Colt. If he couldn't get any answers, Branch damned sure wouldn't be able to get any.

The front entrance was locked, so Colt went around to the back. Three guys, stockers, bartenders or kitchen help, stood around in a huddle smoking. They looked up and called out greetings.

"Afternoon," he said. "Is Beth working?" He knew she was because he had dropped by the trailer park where she lived. She hadn't been home and her neighbor had said she was at work.

"She's getting tables ready." One of the men jerked his head toward the employee entrance. "Go on in, Sheriff. Ray Stokes, the manager, is in there, too."

Colt gave the man a nod of thanks. Stokes wasn't exactly a friend. Evidently the man who'd warned him that Stokes was inside knew as much.

Back in his early deputy days Colt had hauled Stokes in for drunk-and-disorderly charges on several occasions. Stokes had settled down eventually and taken over managing this place when it changed owners. The current owner lived up around Nashville and likely didn't know Stokes was a knucklehead and plain old pain in the ass.

The walk through the stockroom and the kitchen took all of twenty seconds and already Stokes was waiting at the end of the bar. Evidently his man outside had called or sent him a text warning that Colt was on his way inside.

"Evening, Sheriff." Stokes stood, feet wide apart, arms at his side, braced for whatever was coming.

Colt set his hands on his hips and eyed the man speculatively. "You expecting trouble, Ace?" Back in the day Stokes went by the nickname Ace because no matter how deep into trouble he managed to dig himself, he always seemed to have an ace up his sleeve to salvage the situation.

"When I hear the law is sniffing around before I even open, it can be a little troubling. Do we have a problem, Colt?"

Colt shook his head. "Not to my knowledge. I just dropped by to talk to Beth." He gestured to the lady pulling down stools and stationing them around the tables.

Stokes glanced at Beth and then narrowed his

gaze at Colt. "Long as you don't slow down her work, I got no problem with you talking to her. I do need her on shift tonight, so if you're planning to haul her in, I'd ask that you come back after midnight."

"I don't have a beef with Beth, either. Just need to ask her some questions."

"Leave him alone, Ray," Beth called out to her boss. "Come on over here, Colt, so I can keep working."

Stokes shot Colt one last glare before moving back behind the bar that snaked around two sides of the enormous space. The ceiling soared upward at least thirty or so feet. What was once an arena for showing off livestock was now a massive dance floor with a center stage. Tables surrounded the dance floor, filling the rest of the space all the way to the outer walls. There were two emergency exits, a main entrance and the rear one Colt had walked through. Lights and speakers hung in the enormous open space overhead.

"Let me guess," she said as he approached, "you're here to ask me about Sarah's husband."

Colt grabbed a stool from where it sat seat-down on top of the table, settled it onto its legs and tucked it in. "You've been keeping up with the news."

"It's not every day that my big sister shoots

a man dead." She moved on to the next table. Colt followed.

"I guess she did what she had to do." He reached for another stool. "What can you tell me about her husband?"

Beth laughed. "You're forgetting I was exiled from the family long before Sarah married Wesley."

"No, ma'am," Colt countered, "I haven't forgotten. I just figured sisters have a bond, you know? Maybe the two of you talk from time to time with or without your daddy's approval."

Most kids broke the rules occasionally, particularly once they were grown up. Parents' wishes weren't always followed to the letter. God knows he didn't always do what his daddy told him to or he would never have gotten off onto the wrong path in the first place. He sure wished he could make Key see that as much as he resented Colt's guidance, age and experience made a man wise. He should defer to wisdom.

Kids never wanted to go there. Some things they had to learn themselves.

"We talk," Beth admitted.

She continued pulling down stools, placing them just so and then moving on. Colt did the same. He waited as patiently as possible for her to continue. Not exactly the easiest thing to do with the minutes ticking like bombs in his head.

"When she met Wesley, I was still in Nashville. She was so excited. He was way older than her and so charming." Beth hesitated, her expression distant, remembering. "She said he'd lived in the big city most of his life and that he was the most thoughtful man she had ever met."

"Did her opinion of him change over time?" Colt couldn't help wondering if the man was able to repress his criminal side so thoroughly. But then he'd been an accountant, not a killer.

"No. She has never complained about him even once. He has been the perfect husband and father. Kind, generous with his time and affection. Faithful."

Colt focused on the stools as she went on. His guilt prevented him from making eye contact for a half a minute or so. He'd failed on that last one. And even eighteen years later he felt the shame of it.

"Poppa was taken with him as well. He saw Wesley as the kind of strong leader the community would need in coming years."

"But something went wrong." Colt followed her to the next table. "Mr. Yoder learned Wesley's secret."

Beth nodded. "A family from Markham—the town Wesley claimed as his home—paid a visit to Winchester for the funeral of a distant relative. Wesley couldn't possibly have known that anyone in Markham knew anyone in Winchester, much less was distantly related. The folks who visited were quite shocked to learn that the Wesley Sauder they'd buried a decade before was alive and well in Winchester."

Branch had told him most of that part. He likely didn't know about the family who had visited Winchester and outed Wesley. "So Sarah's husband had assumed a dead man's identity." Happened a lot. Generally not so literally. More often just online for credit or tax purposes. But like Branch said, this guy had needed a whole new life. And being an accountant he knew the ins and outs of making his new identity legit.

"How is it that Mr. Yoder kept this news to himself, since it obviously happened a couple of months ago? Rumor is, he and Wesley had their falling-out right after Christmas."

"My poppa is a thorough man. He wanted to see for himself if what this family said was true so he sent my oldest brother, Ben, to Markham to get the whole story. This was just last month. When Ben returned with the confirmation of what they'd been told, Poppa was ready to call a meeting and throw Wesley under the bus, but something stopped him."

She moved through the arrangement of four

more barstools without speaking. Colt nudged, "What do you think stopped him?"

Beth paused and met Colt's gaze. "I can't tell you that part, Sheriff."

He had a feeling the part she didn't want to talk about involved her brother. "Beth, the only thing I want to do in all this is protect the community. Two men are dead. Both of them probably deserved what they got, but we might not be so lucky next time. Next time an innocent person could die. Sarah or one of her children. Whatever you're holding back, I promise you if you give me the whole story I'll do everything in my power to protect you and whoever it is you're protecting if possible."

She reached for another stool. "Benjamin did more than take a picture of the grave and visit the congregation where he found a photo of the deceased Wesley Sauder. He had a picture of Sarah's Wesley with him. He went around asking people if they knew him. 'Course he didn't find anyone who admitted to knowing Sarah's husband. But Sarah and I think it was him showing that picture around that brought all this down on Wesley."

Unfortunately, Sarah and Beth were most likely right. Ben probably showed the photo to the wrong person on the street and word got back to the head of the Cicero family that the missing accountant was in Winchester posing as the Mennonite Wesley Sauder.

"Was Ben or Mr. Yoder contacted by anyone?" Though they had no phone at home, there was a phone at the bakery. The bakery was listed under the Yoder name.

"Sarah said she received several strange calls. The caller would ask for someone named Bateman. She told them they had the wrong number. But when she told Wesley the other day, he went crazy. Told her he had to get out of town. He warned her to keep the shotgun close whenever she was at home and to take it to the bakery with her. This was last week. Then he disappeared. Just took off, claiming he needed to see after the family of some friend who had died. Sarah was seriously upset."

Colt paused. "When did Wesley get back?"

Beth released a big breath. "Not until yesterday."

Which meant he wasn't in Winchester on Monday night. Wesley Sauder—aka Thomas Bateman—couldn't have killed the man in the storeroom at the bakery. Oh hell. "Beth, what happened at the bakery?"

She stared directly at him then. "Sarah called me. She was alone at the bakery. They're closed on Sundays, you know. She was cleaning, stocking. The kids were there, too. She wanted to talk.

She was scared. She thought someone had been following her."

Holy hell.

"She was right, someone was following her. He walked around the building. She saw him through a window so she hid the children behind some boxes in the walk-in cooler. The next thing she knew the man was inside. She'd forgotten to lock the back entrance. He was demanding to know where Wesley was. She kept telling him she didn't know but he wouldn't listen. He backed her into the storeroom." Tears slid down her cheeks. "He was going to kill her, Colt."

"But you got there just in the nick of time."

She nodded. "I brought my .38 with me, just in case. I never expected to have to use it." Her lips trembled. "When I told him to stop, he turned around and the only reason I'm not dead is because I shot first."

The words rang in the air for an endless beat. "It was self-defense, Beth. If you hadn't shot him, you and Sarah and the kids would be dead."

She nodded, swiped at her cheeks. "I guess you have to arrest me now."

Colt shook his head. "No. I'm not going to arrest you for defending yourself. But I will need a statement, and I'll need one from Sarah confirming what you've told me."

"Okay. I'll finish up here first, if that's okay."

"Sure. I'll help you." They moved to the next table. "I'll also need the gun you used."

"It's buried in the flower bed in front of my trailer."

"When we leave I'll call my evidence tech and have him go by and pick it up if I have your permission."

"Do what you have to do," she agreed. "I'm trusting you, Colt. I screwed up my life once, but this time I did the right thing. Don't punish me for doing the right thing."

The fear and resignation in her voice tugged at his protective instincts. He could only imagine how terrified she had been when he walked in a little while ago. "I'll see to it that no one punishes you for this, Beth. I just wish you'd come to me."

She nodded. "I know. It was a dumb decision to try to cover up what I'd done. I guess after everything else I've screwed up, I couldn't deal with my family thinking I was a killer, too."

"You're not a killer, Beth." Colt touched her arm when she reached for another stool. "You're a hero. You saved your sister's life and the lives of her children. Your daddy will be proud when he hears about that."

More tears spilled down her cheeks. "Maybe."

"Tell me how I'm going to find Wesley before his old friends do. I know he's close, hiding out within the Mennonite community, but none of his friends will tell me anything."

"They're protecting him," Beth confirmed. "They know him as Wesley Sauder, the good man who saved my poppa's life. He's been especially helpful to their community. They're not going to easily accept that he's not who he's claimed to be all this time."

"So they're not going to talk to me."

"Probably not." She smiled across the table at Colt. "But one of their wives might. Go see Jenny Hoover. Tell her I sent you." A frown lined her brow. "But you'll need to take a woman with you. I'd say I would go, but if anyone sees me that could get her into trouble." Her expression brightened. "Take Audrey Anderson. Everyone knows her. Jenny will talk to Audrey."

Sounded easy enough.

All Colt had to do first was get Beth out of here without having to kick Ray Stokes's ass.

Chapter Thirteen

Audrey left the office once the paper was put to bed. She needed to visit her mom again. It likely wouldn't do any good, but she had to try. She had a name now, though she wasn't sure that would help in any way. She had tried all afternoon to piece together the shattered memories. But too many fragments were missing.

Basically she had been a child when it happened. Time had done its job, putting distance between her and the trauma. Her mind had buried so much of that night that her recall was no more reliable than her mom's. But she had to try to remember. What happened when she was twelve years old had some bearing, however remote, on what was happening now. She was certain of it.

There was a connection.

What if Wesley Sauder or Thomas Bateman, whatever name he went by, hadn't come to Winchester by chance? Would he know why Jack Torrino had shown up in her father's office all those years ago?

Had Sauder passed the newspaper offices every day for the past ten years knowing the Anderson secret? Audrey had to talk to him before he was hauled away by Branch or killed by another mob thug.

She needed the truth.

But what if the truth was not what she believed it to be? What if her father had somehow been involved in organized crime?

"No way." She would not believe such a thing. Surely her mom or Uncle Phil would have known something was going on if that were the case.

Or perhaps her mom had urged her to forget that night because there was something more unseemly going on?

Her fingers tightened on the steering wheel. She had no idea where she was going. Out of town, along the back roads. Wesley Sauder was hiding somewhere and she intended to find him. She needed answers. The not knowing was driving her mad. The rain had stayed away so far, but it was supposed to start up again later tonight. He had to be lying low somewhere.

As if she'd telegraphed the thought to local law enforcement, blue lights appeared in her rearview mirror. She frowned. The truck was Colt's. Why would he be blue-lighting her? She glanced at the dash. She wasn't speeding.

Cursing her bad luck, she pulled to the curb and put the car in Park. Then she waited. If he asked to see her license she was going to punch him.

He swaggered up to her window. She watched each step in her side mirror, her pulse reacting. Why didn't her libido just die? Experiencing all the sudden urges for Colt was making her crazy. She did not want to repeat the same mistake she'd made as a kid. She'd given him too much of her life already.

When he braced his hands on the roof of the car and peered down at her, she powered down the window. "Was I speeding, Sheriff?"

"No, ma'am." He moved down to the window then, propping his crossed arms there. "Why aren't you answering your cell?"

Her cell hadn't rung? She poked a hand into her bag and retrieved her phone. Three missed calls. "I didn't hear it ring." She checked the sound— it was off. "Oh." She switched the setting from mute. "Sorry, I was in a meeting. I just forgot to turn on the ringer when I left the paper."

The truth was she was so distracted and frustrated she hadn't even thought about her phone.

"I need you to take a ride with me, if you will."

Her heart stumbled. Did he already know about Torrino? How the hell had he figured it out? Judd would never tell anyone about her questions and even if he did, there was no way to take her questions and follow them back to anything related to her parents or the newspaper, much less that damned basement.

"Why?" Her voice was a little too high-pitched.

"I want to interview Jenny Hoover. Sarah's younger sister Beth thinks Jenny's husband might know where Sauder is. He won't tell me, but Beth thinks Jenny will talk. To *you*."

Audrey vaguely remembered Jenny Hoover; she had been Jenny Kauffman back when they were kids. If talking to Jenny would help Audrey find Sauder, she was more than happy to do so. But she and Colt had to get one thing straight first. "On one condition."

"I let you have the exclusive," he said with a shrug. "You got it. I've already promised you the exclusive."

She shook her head. "I need to ask Sauder a couple of questions before you turn him over to Branch."

Colt drew back the slightest bit. "Do you mean privately or in my presence?"

She chewed her lip. "Privately."

"I don't know about that, Rey. There are all kinds of rules about witnesses and—"

"Two minutes, that's all I'll need."

Big exhale. "All right. As long as it's within my

power to allow, you will have two minutes. Can we leave my truck at your house? I don't want to spook Jenny by showing up in my vehicle, particularly at this hour."

He was right. It was half past eight. "Of course."

"Great." He smiled. "I knew I could count on you, Rey."

He might not feel that way when he learned the secret she and her mother had been hiding for more than two decades. Reminding herself to breathe, Audrey drove to her house. Colt parked his truck and hustled over to climb into her passenger seat.

"What if Jenny's husband is home?"

"Beth says Wednesday nights are meeting night for the men. They'll be at the church until after ten."

"I imagine Sauder is too smart to be there with them."

"If he's not, then I don't know how he was ever an accountant for a crime family."

Audrey laughed, couldn't help herself. "You have a point."

En route to the Hoover home they drove past the Mennonite church, and there was quite the crowd of vehicles there. Some sort of meeting was certainly taking place tonight. The Hoover farm was on Walnut Grove Road. Like the Yoder place, this one had been in the family for several generations. Since the first Mennonites came to the area, actually.

Colt followed Audrey across the yard and up the steps onto the porch. He took a position to one side of the door as she pulled open the screen door and knocked on the wood one beyond it. The lacy curtains in the window had moved twice. Jenny or one of her children already knew they had company. It was quiet inside. Audrey knocked again. Hearing the sound of footsteps inside, she allowed the screen door to close. Another day was all but gone and still no sign of Sauder. It seemed impossible that a fugitive could stay hidden like this in such a small town with every cop in the various law enforcement agencies looking for him.

The door opened and Jenny peered through the screen door. "You're Audrey Anderson."

Audrey smiled. "In the flesh."

Jenny glanced at Colt and her awed expression slipped. "Sheriff."

"I realize it's really late but if you have time," Audrey said quickly, not wanting to lose this chance because the woman got hung up on the idea that Colt was now standing next to her, "I would love to talk to you for a few minutes. Beth Yoder sent me."

Jenny's attention rested on Audrey once more and that fangirl expression was back. "All right."

She stepped back, opening the door wider. "Would you like a cup of tea?"

Audrey gave her the brightest smile she could muster. "Tea would be lovely."

"The kitchen is this way," she said, ushering Audrey across the room.

Audrey heard the front door close and then the steady fall of Colt's steps as he followed them into the large but simple kitchen.

"How are your girls?" Audrey asked as Jenny put the teakettle on the stove and lit the burner under it. "I saw their artwork on the wall at the bakery. They're both very talented."

Jenny blushed as she settled white cups into saucers. "They're doing well. Ana is getting married this summer and Ruth is traveling to Virginia to spend the summer with her grandmother. It's going to be an exciting summer for them, but certainly a long one for me without my girls."

Audrey kept her opinions to herself about how two such talented young ladies should be heading off to college. She had no right to judge and certainly no grounds upon which to suggest how anyone should raise her children.

"I would love to do an article about the wedding, if you and your husband would permit me."

The other woman's eyes danced with obvious delight. "I'll ask him. He'll be home later in an hour or so."

"I think it would be a lovely local life piece."

The kettle whistled and Jenny prepared the tea. When they had settled around the kitchen table, Jenny said, "I guess you came to ask me about Sarah's husband."

Audrey nodded. "We're really worried about him. More of those bad guys could show up at any moment—they may already be here—and we need to find him before they do. If you can help, you would be doing Sarah and her children a great favor. The truth is, they're in danger, too. I can't emphasize enough how important it is that Sheriff Tanner find Wesley and help him. I really believe he's the only one who can give Wesley a fair shake in this mess."

Jenny nodded. "I told Allan we should talk to Sheriff Tanner." She glanced at him, her first concession to his presence since they gathered at the table. "But he wouldn't listen."

"Men always think they know best." Audrey shook her head. "I'll never understand that mentality."

Jenny sighed. "It's a burden at times."

"Do you know where Wesley is staying?" Audrey asked. "You have my word that Sheriff Tanner will protect him. Whatever you tell us will go no further than this room."

"Mine as well," Colt offered. "Wesley Sauder

is my responsibility to protect. But I can't do my job if I don't know where he is."

"The last I heard Allen say, he was staying at the Zimmerman place." She looked from Audrey to Colt and back. "But he's moved and no one is talking. I honestly don't know where he is."

As disappointing as it was, Audrey believed her. "If you had to guess, where would you start your search for Wesley?"

The other woman looked Audrey straight in the eye and said, "At his house."

Audrey was surprised by her answer, then the rationale behind it dawned on her. No one would be watching his house. They were all too busy looking everywhere else. "Thank you, Jenny. You've been a tremendous help."

They finished their tea in record time and Colt thanked Jenny as she walked them to the door. She nodded but said nothing else to him. To Audrey she said, "I love your newspaper, Ms. Anderson. A lot of us live vicariously through you and the introspections column you do about all the places you've visited and the things you've done."

Now that was a compliment. She'd only started that column because Brian insisted. She supposed he'd been right to encourage her in that direction. "Thank you, Jenny. It really was nice to see you again."

At the car Colt held the door for her, then shut

it once she was behind the wheel. He rounded the hood and slid into the passenger seat. "There's just one problem with her theory," he said as he pulled the seat belt across his lap.

"What's that?" Audrey snapped her seat belt into place and started the engine. She looked at him and waited for an answer.

"I've had a deputy watching the Sauder home since Sarah went back there."

Audrey guided the car down the drive and onto the dark road. "What if he was already back in the house before you assigned surveillance? What if…" She braked and looked at him across the dim glow of the dash. "What if he never left the house?"

"I saw him running from the Zimmerman house." Colt countered.

"Did you, or did you see someone who looked like him?"

His brow furrowed in concentration. "God Almighty, you could be right." Colt shook his head. "I kept asking myself how any man could leave his wife and children alone to save his own life. Maybe he didn't."

Audrey drove as fast as she dared on the twisty back roads between the Hoover place and the Sauder home. Colt had a death grip on the armrest of the door but he didn't caution her to slow down even once.

The dark house looming at the end of the driveway was a huge disappointment. Colt got out and knocked anyway, but no one was home. Without a warrant he couldn't go in, not since the house had been released and was no longer considered an official crime scene.

Warrant or no, Colt walked around the house, checking the barn and the smokehouse. Both were open. Audrey followed along behind him, mostly because she had no desire to sit in the car in the dark all alone. He walked out to the road and spoke to the deputy in the cruiser watching over the house. Audrey stared at the dark windows. She couldn't help wondering again if Wesley Sauder knew anything about the man who'd given her father trouble all those years ago.

"Sarah and the kids haven't been back over here tonight," Colt said as he joined her at her car. "If you don't mind, take me back to my truck and I'll pay the Yoders a visit. See if Sarah and her kids are over there."

"I can take you there." She was certainly in no hurry to get home to an empty house. When she put it that way it sounded so sad. For the past six months she'd lived alone in that old house without thinking too much about being lonely. Suddenly that was all she could think about.

"If you're sure you don't mind."

"I don't mind. Really. It's no problem. Besides,

it's already so late we should do this the most efficient way possible."

"Good point."

They rode in silence. Audrey couldn't stop obsessing about the man, Jack Torrino, who had disappeared. What if Sauder couldn't shed any light on why he had come to Winchester? Where did she go from there with her questions?

There was always hypnosis therapy to see if anything could be excavated from her head. Did she really want to risk allowing a doctor, despite being bound by confidentiality, to hear what really happened that night? Would it be better just to leave the past in the past?

She just didn't know anymore.

The stop at the Yoder home proved futile as well. The children were there, tucked in for the night, but Sarah Sauder wasn't at her father's house. Aaron insisted he had not seen her since she left to return home when her house was released.

"Where to now?" Audrey asked Colt once they were back in her car.

"Let's call it a night. I need to think on this some more and regroup in the morning."

"You're the boss."

"I'm sorry about asking you to dinner tonight and then dragging you into all this instead."

She flashed him a smile. "It's okay. We can have dinner another time."

An entire minute passed with him staring at her profile. She didn't have to turn toward him and it didn't matter that it was dark in the vehicle save for the dash lights. She could feel him watching her.

"What?" she finally demanded.

"Do you mean that?"

She started to ask what he was talking about and then she realized what she had said. "Of course I meant it. We all have to eat sometime. No reason friends can't have dinner."

"Okay."

That one word—four letters—whispered through the darkness like a caress. How could she feel all these confusing emotions at a time like this? Or maybe they were just her mind's way of trying to escape what was happening. But there was no escaping. This case was about to explode and the big secret she and her mother had been keeping all these years was going to be amid the rubble.

Audrey drove through the darkness, her mind drifting back to the things she did not want to think about but had no choice. She had lived with this secret for twenty-three years, eleven months and about two weeks—why couldn't she just let it go? Hope and pray that this investigation would somehow skirt right on past her family and the newspaper?

She would never be that lucky.

"Rey?"

She turned to Colt, blinked. "Yeah?"

"We've been sitting at this stop sign for two whole minutes."

"Oh. I'm sorry." She shook her head, checked both directions, then prepared to pull across the intersection. "I was a million miles away."

"I figured."

More of that silence settled around them as she drove to her house. She'd pulled into the driveway and parked next to Colt's truck before he spoke again. "Thanks for chauffeuring me around and helping with Jenny Hoover."

"I wish we'd found him." She climbed out of the car. When he'd done the same she locked it with her key fob. "Maybe tomorrow."

The porch light was on but it didn't quite reach this part of the driveway. She walked beside him to his truck. The moon was bright enough for her to see his face and the weariness there. This was his county and he was worried about the safety of all the residents. As worried about her own problems as she was, she could only imagine the burden he carried.

"Maybe tomorrow," he agreed.

"Good night, Colt."

When she would have turned away, he touched her arm. "I'm glad we've spent some time together the past couple of days, despite the circumstances. It's been nice."

As much as she wanted to make some flippant remark and walk away, she couldn't do it. Not now. He needed her support and he was right. "It has been nice. I don't want to go back to avoiding each other. I want to be friends." There, she'd said it. What was more, she meant it.

He smiled and her heart swelled so big she couldn't breathe.

"I will take being friends, Rey, but I have to be completely honest with you. I will always dream of more."

Maybe if he'd said he wanted more or needed more she might have been able to simply turn around and go into the house. But he said dream… he would always dream of more.

She went up on her tiptoes and kissed him on the jaw. "Night."

His arms went around her waist before she could move away and he pulled her to him. His lips landed on hers and he kissed her so softly, so sweetly that she thought she might cry. Instead, she melted against him and he deepened the kiss.

When she could endure the tenderness no longer without dragging him inside and to her bed, she drew back. "Drive safely."

"I will. G'night."

She hurried up the steps and to the door. He watched until she'd unlocked it and gone inside, then he drove away. She observed from the window until his taillights disappeared into the darkness.

That was the moment when she understood she could never again pretend there was nothing left between them. There would always be something wonderful, something special between them. All they had to do was find a way to work it into who they were today.

Her cell rang, drawing her back to the here and now. She dragged it from her bag and tapped the screen without even checking to see who had called. "Anderson."

"Rey, you have to come to the office."

Brian. "What's wrong?" He sounded frantic, upset…worried.

"The basement has flooded. The water is knee-deep and rising. I was able to get a contractor over here and he's trying to get the water stopped. But he has to dig up…"

Audrey didn't hear the rest of what he said. She was running back to her car. She had to get to the newspaper. *Now.*

She had to stop the digging…

Before it was too late.

Chapter Fourteen

Colt had no sooner left Rey's place than his cell vibrated against his belt. He tugged it from its holder. Didn't recognize the number.

"Colt Tanner."

"Sheriff, this is Wesley Sauder."

Colt slowed for the turn onto his street. He tempered his tone and chose his words carefully. "Mr. Sauder, I'm glad you called. I want to help you, but we need to talk as soon as possible."

"I don't have time for talking right now, Sheriff. They've got Sarah."

Worry twisted in Colt's gut. "Tell me where you are and I'll come right now."

"I'm at our home. Hurry, Sheriff. I can only talk to you. I can't trust anyone else. Especially not any of the Feds. Just you, please."

"On my way, Sauder." Doing a one-eighty, Colt punched the accelerator and headed for Buncombe Road. "Is it safe for you to stay in the house?"

"I'm in a hidden safe room. I'll stay in here until you get here."

No wonder they hadn't been able to find the man. Colt should have thought of that sooner. A man like that, who never knew when his past was going to catch up to him, would take certain precautions. There was likely a hidden space between closets or rooms. Rey had been right. Sauder was likely at home all along. Considering that revelation, Colt wondered if Wesley was the one who shot Marcello instead of Sarah?

"Damn it, Sauder," he muttered. Hopefully the kids would be safe at the Yoder place, but Sarah could end up dead.

Colt gunned the engine for all it was worth. The sooner he was there, the sooner he could properly assess the situation. His first instinct was to call Branch, but he hesitated. Sauder wanted him to come alone. Could be a setup, but he didn't see the point. If the mob thugs had Sauder, they would take him out or take him back to Chicago; the end result would be the same either way. They wouldn't waste time on Colt—some small-town sheriff who knew nothing about them or their organization was no threat.

The promise he'd made to Rey would have to wait. Whatever was happening with Sauder right now, it was too dangerous to involve her. There was already one too many potential victims for his liking. He sure as hell wasn't bringing anyone else into this dangerous situation. His best bet was to get the lay of the land and go from there.

Before he could stop himself he thought of the way Rey had kissed him and then the way he had kissed her back. As much as he wanted to he couldn't analyze that kiss right now or the fact that she'd kissed him first. How very much he wanted to do more than kiss her would have to wait. He'd hurt her badly. It would take time to regain her trust all the way. He had waited a very long time already to have a second chance, but patience was required if they were going to continue moving forward. He refused to allow anything outside a life-and-death situation—like this one—to get in the way.

When this was over, he and Rey would see where this first step took them.

The drive to the Sauder home took a full ten minutes despite his best efforts. Colt pulled into the drive and skidded to a stop. He walked straight over to Deputy Avans, who was tonight's surveillance detail.

"You can take a break, Deputy. I'll be here for a half hour or so."

"You sure, Sheriff?" He looked from Colt to the house and back.

Colt slapped the roof of the car. "I'm sure. Go. Come back in half an hour."

"Yes, sir."

Avans was concerned. He didn't want to go, but he did as he was ordered. When he was out of sight, Colt crossed the road and walked straight to the front door of the house. The door opened and Sauder stayed behind it in the darkness. As soon as Colt was across the threshold, the door closed, leaving the room in total darkness.

"This way, Sheriff."

Colt blinked as his eyes adjusted to the darkness. He followed Sauder into the center hallway, away from rooms with windows. A lit candle sat on a narrow table. He turned to Colt, his face pinched in fear.

"They told me if I turned myself over to them, they would release Sarah. I'll do whatever I have to do, no question about that, but I don't trust them to stick to their word."

"Are the kids safe where they are?"

"Yes. Benjamin and Aaron are watching for trouble. I've warned them not to allow anyone to get close to the house. I've also alerted several neighbors who are keeping an eye out around the Yoder farm."

"I have most of the story, Wesley," Colt said, keeping the conversation friendly, just two neighbors talking. "You were friends with Louis Cicero's son. You went to college together and later you were hired by his father. But it was your friend's sister that changed everything."

He nodded. "I was in love with Sophia. We wanted to get married but her father had decided she would marry the son of someone who would provide good business alliances. It's the way of things in that world. Alliances are often made with marriages. Sophia went behind his back—mine, too—and started talking to the FBI. She told me she was going to find a way out for us. I had no idea what she had in mind or I would have stopped her. Not that I wanted to protect her father—certainly not—but I understood the move was suicide. By the time she told me what she'd done it was too late. I could join her or end up on the wrong side of the sting. Of course I joined her."

"You believe Louis Cicero killed her."

"I know he killed her. Her brother told me. He was devastated. But what could he do? The man is his father and he knew his future depended on which side he chose. He chose his father's. Family is everything and she betrayed them. I pretended to go along with their thinking. No one knew Sophia and I were in love or that we had gone to the FBI together. First chance I got, I took a little insurance and I disappeared."

"You assumed someone else's identity and burrowed into a community where you would be protected as long as you were accepted." This was the one part that bugged the hell out of Colt. He remembered Melvin Yoder's accident. The possibility that this guy could have somehow masterminded the accident wasn't lost on him considering all that he knew now. "You took advantage of an awfully convenient situation to get your foot in the door."

Sauder frowned. "Are you talking about what happened to Melvin all those years ago?"

"It was a mighty big coincidence."

"You should ask Ezra," Sauder offered. "He was supposed to be there with Melvin that day but he forgot. When Melvin got into trouble with that bull, he didn't have the help he needed. It was sheer luck I came along when I did." He gave a somber nod. "Melvin and I never told anyone Ezra let him down. He made a mistake. It was best to let it go."

Colt was glad to hear it. He hadn't wanted to believe Sauder had fooled everyone so thoroughly.

"I'm a criminal, that's true," Sauder went on. "I worked for a man operating one of the largest organized crime families in the country. I did what he told me to do. But it was all on paper. The tools of my trade were a calculator and a computer. I'm not a killer, Sheriff. I'm just a man who was a fool when he was younger and I've spent the past ten-plus years doing everything within my power to make up for it."

Colt's father had often spoken of the good work Wesley Sauder had done for the community, and not just the Mennonite community.

"Why didn't you take the evidence to the Feds and ruin Cicero?" Colt countered. "He murdered the woman you loved. How could you disappear and start over without avenging her death?" The question had to be asked. Sauder might be a good man now but he'd obviously been a coward then.

Sauder dropped his gaze for a moment before meeting Colt's. "How do you think the old man found out what Sophia had done?"

The question stunned Colt for a moment. "Are you suggesting someone in the FBI's Chicago office told him?"

"I'm not suggesting anything," he argued. "I'm telling you that's what happened."

"Do you know who it was?"

"I do. He's a big shot in the DC office now."

"Can you prove that allegation?"

"I can and I will. Just help me get my wife back."

Colt nodded. "Do you know how many we're up against?"

"Doesn't matter. I'm ready to turn myself over to them and take whatever they have planned for me. If I'd thought for a second they would stick by their word, I would have done it already. All I need you to do is make sure Sarah gets away safely. Nothing else matters to me."

"You know they'll kill you."

"I'm sure they'll torture me first. They'll want to make an example of me before they're done. As long as Sarah and the children are okay, they can do whatever they like to me."

He was either telling the truth or he was the best damn liar Colt had ever encountered. "Well, all right then. There's just one problem. As much as I'd like to play the hero, I know my limitations, Wesley, and I think you know your own. We're going to need the right kind of backup."

He nodded reluctantly. "I guess you're right." He covered his face with his hands. "I just don't want them to hurt her."

"We're going to do everything possible to make sure that doesn't happen."

Colt called Deputy Avans and had him come into the house. He used the excuse that the back door lock was broken. He met him in the living area. No need for the deputy to see Sauder and get excited. He was fairly new in the department.

"I'm concerned about who may have come into the house without our knowledge," he told the young man. "I want you to track down Branch Holloway and tell him to meet me here. Tell him to hurry. He and I need to talk."

"Yes, sir."

When Avans was gone, Colt locked the door and returned to the hall where Sauder was pacing.

"Now, let's go over exactly what happened. Sarah wasn't at her father's house when I went by there tonight. The kids were there but Aaron claimed he hadn't seen her since she came back home after we released this house."

Sauder nodded. "We didn't want to risk the kids getting pulled into this, so she left them with her father and brothers. She was going to see them and then come straight back. I didn't want her to go, but she said she had to see her babies. She never made it to Melvin's house."

"I've had this house under surveillance. Sarah hasn't been here, either."

He shrugged. "We have an underground tunnel from the barn into the safe room between the two bedroom closets. We've been staying in the tunnel most of the time except when Sarah went to the bakery or to visit the kids. We wanted anyone who was watching to believe that I was gone. Tonight we decided to get the evidence I've had hidden for all these years. We were going to offer it to them if they would just leave us alone. But our plan was too late."

"So the man or men who have Sarah know you're close."

Sauder nodded. "He wants me to bring the evidence to him. He'll let Sarah go and I go back to Chicago with him. That's the deal he offered and I accepted. I just need you to ensure he holds up his end of the bargain."

"Are you certain it's just one man?"

He nodded. "There were three when they first showed up on Monday evening. This one is Saul the Saw. He's one of the most experienced and most ruthless hit men in the family, but he hasn't done the dirty work himself in a long time. I'm sure the old man sent him just to be sure the job got done. With the other two out, Saul has no choice but to finish this personally. He never fails, Sheriff. Never. There's no way he's going back to Chicago without me. He would kill himself first."

Suited Colt just fine. He would be more than happy for Saul the Saw to end up in the county morgue or for him to spend the rest of his days in Nashville's federal prison.

"Well then, let's go rescue your wife, Sauder."

Chapter Fifteen

Audrey was ready to scream by the time the officer finally strolled up to her window and handed her the speeding ticket. How was she supposed to get to the newspaper and stop the travesty playing out there parked at the curb waiting for this officer to do his duty?

When he leaned down once more she clamped her jaw shut to keep from spewing those very words at him.

"The court date is at the bottom," he informed her. "You be sure to pay your ticket before that date or make the scheduled appearance."

Audrey continued to hold back the rant she wanted to make. She would be calling Chief of Police Billy Brannigan about how long it took one of his officers to write a damned ticket. She'd almost lost her mind waiting on the man.

"I'll be sure to do that, Officer."

"You slow down, Ms. Anderson. You're lucky I was feeling generous and just gave you a speeding ticket. You can't be driving sixty in a thirty-mile-an-hour zone."

"I'm so sorry. As I said there's an emergency at the paper." She could literally see the newspaper building from where she was sitting. If she'd only made it another block before he noticed her, she wouldn't be patiently sitting here forcing a smile she in no way felt. She silently urged him to walk away…to get back in his cruiser and be gone before she imploded.

"Have a nice night, ma'am." He tipped his head and sauntered on back to his cruiser.

"You, too, Officer."

Probably all of his speeding stops had excuses. But hers was real. She swallowed hard as she shifted into Drive and rolled forward. As much as she wanted to stomp the accelerator and fly the final few hundred yards, she was well aware the officer would be watching. So she drove the speed limit, made the turn onto the street adjacent to the newspaper and then the final turn, a left, into the rear parking lot.

Her heart sank as she spotted the plumbing contractor's truck. She parked, scrambled out of her car and rushed into the building through the rear entrance, which was already unlocked. The door was blocked with a rubber shim to keep it from closing and locking out anyone who needed access.

If she was too late… God, she did not even want to think that way.

She reached the door to the basement and it swung open before she could grab the knob.

At the sight of her, Brian grabbed his chest. "You scared the hell out of me."

"What's going on down there?" Suddenly she didn't want to go down those stairs. Flashes of memories from that night zoomed through her mind like lightning strikes. Her mother crying. Her father dead on the floor in his office…and the other man. Oh God, the other man had been dead, too. Shot in the chest. Blood everywhere. Scrubbing the wood floor in her father's office.

She put a hand to her stomach to stop the roiling there. Oh God.

"The water just kept getting deeper and deeper." Brian shuddered. "I moved everything up to the higher shelves while the contractor was trying to figure out how to get the water turned off. Apparently our main shutoff failed and they had to find the nearest shutoff the city installed for the block. Do you know how complicated that was? This building—this whole block—is so old no one knew where to look." His eyes rounded and he spread his arms wide. "The blueprints had been modified so many times it was impossible to make sense of them."

Audrey held up her hands. "Just tell me they got the water shut off."

He nodded. "Finally. Now the fire department is on the way here. They're going to pump the water out of the basement and then we'll go from there."

Her heart slid back into her chest and started to beat once more. "I thought you said something about digging."

"Not yet," he said. "Not until the water is pumped out. He's called for jackhammers to break up the concrete."

The back door burst open and two firemen in full turnout gear hustled into the building dragging an endless line of hose behind them.

"Over here," Brian called.

Before Audrey could say anything else or intercede, her lifelong friend showed the firemen down the basement stairwell with their hose that snaked back out the door and to a truck, she supposed, that had pumping capabilities.

This was a mess. It could not happen. No one could dig up the basement under any circumstances. Removing the water she understood; that had to be done. But the rest couldn't happen.

She took a breath. Reached for calm, couldn't find it. She had to stop whatever was planned after the water was pumped out. Maybe she should shut the paper down. With sudden, acute clarity she abruptly understood that was the only answer. She should have done exactly that when she first came home. But the idea of ending her father's legacy out of fear seemed wrong. Besides, she'd used the excuse that she wanted to carry on the family legacy to halt Phillip's deal with the developer.

Now she was in a corner and there was no way out.

Oh God. She didn't want to think what this would do to her mom.

Brian reappeared and she wanted to shake him, to order him to stop this and to let her go home and think. She needed to figure out how to repair the situation before anything else happened. Turn it around somehow.

Audrey summoned her voice, struggled to keep it even. "When the water is removed, let's call it a night and tackle this problem tomorrow. Let the basement dry out." Sounded completely reasonable to her.

"Are you kidding?" Brian looked at her as if she'd lost her mind.

"No," she snapped. "I am too stressed right now to deal with this, Bri. I need… I need to think. To figure all this out."

As if he'd only then realized she was extremely upset, Brian put his hands on her arms and said, "Audrey, I know you've got some sort of issue with the basement, but this has to be taken care of tonight. We don't have a choice in the matter."

"Why?" she demanded, her worry instantly morphing into irritation. This was her building; if she wanted to stop the planned repairs, she should be able to make that happen. The notion sounded childish even to her but she couldn't feel any other way at the moment.

"No one beyond this building along the entire block has water now. The city shut it off to prevent the swimming pool forming in the basement from rising to this level. Until the repairs are made here—in this building—the water for the entire block has to stay off."

The reality of what he was saying finally bored its way through the haze of confusion and desperation swaddling her brain. There was no stopping this. All she could do now was hope they wouldn't have to dig in a certain spot.

Except she wasn't a fool. The last time that floor had been opened up it was to work on the underground plumbing, and that was exactly where they would need to dig this time. Defeat tugged at her, made remaining vertical almost impossible. She couldn't stop this.

Not this time.

The pump in the truck outside started to hum and churn. Audrey hugged herself, unable to move. She should go to her office. Call Colt. Call her uncle Phillip. He would need to know what was about to happen. Should she sign the deed to the newspaper back over to him tonight? There was no way to know how long it would take to sort out the legal mess. Would they charge her and her mom? Her mom wasn't mentally fit for trial but she would have been all those years ago.

Did that make a difference?

Audrey just didn't know. Was the fact that she had been a child at the time an asset to her case? Doubtful. Besides, any district attorney worth his salt would want to know why she chose not to tell the truth after becoming an adult. There was no excuse for the decisions she and her mom had made.

When the pump finished drawing out the water, the firemen hustled up from the basement, coiling the hose as they moved. Brian thanked them for their help. Audrey should have said something but she couldn't. She just couldn't. What they were doing would change everything. Would reveal this terrible thing.

More men in work boots carrying large tools and dragging more hoses, these considerably smaller in circumference, rushed in and filed down the stairs. Outside a compressor fired up, the sound wafting into the lobby and reminding her that this was really happening.

Her throat was sand dry. The sound of the jackhammers made her flinch. She tried to settle her trembling body but that wasn't happening this side of the grave. She should just go down there and see what they found. Maybe she'd get lucky and a sinkhole had swallowed up the remains of Jack Torrino.

"I should make coffee," Brian said, dragging her from the disturbing thoughts. "You look ready to collapse."

"I'm okay," she lied.

"The one thing you are not is okay," he argued. "What's going on, Rey? What is it about this basement that freaks you out so badly?"

She shook her head. "I'm okay. We should go down and see what's happening."

"If you're up to it."

"I need to be down there."

Once they were through the door, her hand settled on the iron railing and she steadied herself for what was to come. Slowly, she descended into the massive basement that spread out nearly the entire footprint of the building. As Brian had said, he'd moved all the stored boxes to the higher shelves. She should thank him for taking care of this while she was out searching for Sauder.

How had she ever allowed this to go on so long? When she bought the paper she should have spoken to Colt and told him the whole story. But she'd kept that awful secret, and now the whole world was about to know the ugly truth.

By the time they reached the final step the noise was deafening. The jackhammers were like machine guns firing in automatic mode. What was worse, they were digging exactly where she had known they would. Dozens of knots tightened in her belly.

"Rey, you're shaking."

Brian touched her arm and Audrey faced him. "Brian, there's something you should know."

He leaned closer. "What did you say?"

She put her face to his ear. "Let's go back upstairs where we can talk."

Audrey couldn't get up the stairs fast enough. She suddenly felt cold. She hugged herself and tried to find the best way to tell her friend what she had been keeping secret for better than half her life. He had a right to know. He had been with this paper since finishing grad school. It was wrong to leave him in the dark when all hell was about to break loose.

"What's going on, Audrey?" He searched her face, his eyes filled with worry. "I've never seen you so upset. Not since you learned about your mother's dementia."

"Bri, you remember when my father died. It was a real shock. He seemed as healthy as a horse and then he was dead."

"I do." He sighed. "It was a difficult time for you and your mother."

Audrey smiled, her first of the night. "You were there for me. The best friend anyone could ever want."

He grinned. "Colt was, too, as I recall."

"He was." She thought of that kiss tonight. What in the world had she been thinking? That she was tired of being lonely and holding grudges and pretending she didn't care about him anymore. "I'm not sure I could have gotten through that time without the two of you."

"That's what friends are for." Brian frowned. "I really should make coffee. I think we're going to be here for a while and you look terrible."

He was right. She could wait five more minutes. She'd waited more than twenty years already. "Coffee sounds great."

Down the hall beyond the door to the basement was a break room. Audrey watched her friend's efficient movements as he filled the carafe and then poured the water into the reservoir. A few scoops of Colombian dark roast in a filter, and then he pressed the brew button. Instantly the aroma of smooth, dark coffee filled the air.

He poured two cups, added sugar to his own and then carried the coffee to a table. "Sit. Talk to me."

For a minute, Audrey sipped the warm brew,

grateful all over again for his suggestion. She took a deep breath and began. "That night when Mom found Dad, that wasn't the only thing that happened."

She fell silent again. Grasping for the proper words to say to explain what happened. How in the world could she hope to explain murder?

"I'll need a little more than that, Rey. What else happened that night?"

"Mom and I were worried about Dad. It was well past dinnertime and he hadn't come home. He wasn't answering the phone in his office and Uncle Phillip was out for the evening. Since there was no one else to call to check on him, we drove over here. The building was dark—or it looked that way from the outside."

She savored another sip of coffee before going on. "Mother and I parked and found the back door unlocked, which was very unusual. Since Dad was alone at the paper he would never have left the door unlocked. When we got into the lobby we looked up, seeing his office light. We could see that he was arguing with another man."

Brian lowered his cup to the table as if it suddenly felt too heavy. "What man?"

Audrey shrugged. "I have no idea. Just a man."

"Did your mother go up to the office?" His face warned that the possibility of where this was going had disturbed him.

Audrey nodded. "We hurried up the stairs. She ushered me into Uncle Phil's office and told me to stay put until she returned for me. Then she rushed out. She told me later that when she got to his office, my dad and the other man were struggling. There was a gun on the floor. Mom said she shouted at them to stop. Pleaded with them, but they didn't stop. It was obvious to her that it was the other man who wasn't going to stop. And then—"

"Peterson!"

Brian's name echoed down the hall. He jumped. Put a hand to his chest. "Don't move. I'll be right back."

Audrey felt her body collapse into itself as he hurried from the room. She closed her eyes and tried to slow the spinning in her head.

Vibration in her pocket snapped her eyes open. She dragged her cell from her pocket and checked the screen. She hoped there wasn't a problem with her mom. Could be Colt. She frowned, didn't recognize the number. Then the area code sank in. Chicago. Could be Judd.

She hit accept. "Audrey Anderson."

"Can you repeat your name?"

Audrey frowned, drew the phone back and checked the screen again. Then she said, "Audrey Anderson."

"Ms. Anderson, this is Detective Robert Dickson of the Chicago Police Department."

Frowning, Audrey wandered into the hall, moving toward the door to the basement. The racket had stopped. She could only assume they had finished breaking up the concrete. Had they started to move the debris yet?

"How can I help you, Detective Dickson?"

"You have an acquaintance in Chicago named Judd Seymour?"

"I do. He's a friend and business associate." Her pulse rate accelerated; something dark and terrifying moved inside her. "What's this about, Detective?"

"Ma'am, when was the last time you saw Mr. Seymour?"

Oh God. Something had happened to him. "I haven't seen him in a year or so, but we spoke just this morning."

"Can you tell me the nature of your call?"

Nerves jangling, Audrey held her ground. "I'm afraid I'm going to need to know what's going on before I say more, Detective."

"Ma'am, Judd Seymour is dead. He was murdered in his home office. He spoke to you and then he made a couple of calls to numbers we haven't been able to trace. So I'm going to need you to be as cooperative as possible starting right now."

Judd was murdered only hours after talking to

her about this Torrino guy? Had he contacted the wrong source and that source tipped off someone who didn't want Judd or anyone else digging into the past?

Audrey explained to the detective that she'd called Judd about an old case that might be related to a new one happening in Winchester. She had to be careful because she didn't know how much Colt would want her to share. When she'd answered everything she could answer, the detective reminded her that he would likely need to speak to her again. She assured him she would be happy to cooperate in whatever way necessary.

When the call ended, she called Colt. She got his voice mail. "Hey, it's me. I… I'm at the paper." She turned and walked toward the basement. Whatever was going on down there now it was entirely too quiet. "I need to talk to you. There's something I have—"

The grating sound of a car alarm echoed from the parking lot. Audrey paused, turned back to the rear exit and moved in that direction. The headlights of her car flashed in time with the obnoxious sound.

Her car's alarm was the one going off.

"Damn it. Call me when you can. I need you, Colt."

She ended the call, walked out the door and toward the car. She pulled the fob from her pocket and shut off the alarm. When she was within a few steps of reaching it she noticed the passenger-side window was shattered.

"What the hell?"

A hand snaked around and clamped down on her mouth, yanked her backward against an unyielding chest. Cold, hard steel jammed into her temple. "Scream and you're dead."

Chapter Sixteen

Colt was now officially on Branch's bad side. The marshal was damned ticked off. First because Colt hadn't called him the minute he heard from Sauder, and second because he refused to allow Branch to take charge. As angry as he was, in light of the situation, Branch had put his irritation and frustration aside until this was done.

Saving Sarah Sauder's life had to take priority.

Six of Colt's most trusted deputies had fanned out in the woods behind the Zimmerman property; two more were hidden behind farm equipment between the house and the barn. Colt had made his way through the darkness to the smokehouse only a few yards from the end of the house nearest the back door. He was close enough to kick a rock and hit the back of Ezra Zimmerman's house. Branch was in the hayloft with a sharpshooter set up, night-vision scope included, ready to take out the bad guy if things went south.

Now that they were in place, it was time for

Wesley Sauder to move. Branch had refused to proceed under the radar like this without rigging up a tracking bracelet on Sauder. Colt didn't actually blame him. The FBI and the Marshals Service had looked for Thomas Bateman for a long time. They had him figured for dead. Now that they knew he was still breathing, he wasn't getting away again.

The deal was—assuming everyone survived this operation—Bateman, aka Sauder, would testify against Louis Cicero in exchange for immunity. He and his family would go into witness protection for the rest of their lives. It stunk for Sarah because she had family, but it was the best deal they were going to get.

The old pickup belonging to Sauder rolled into the driveway. Renewed tension poured through Colt. He hoped like hell Sarah made it alive and uninjured through this mess. It would be good if Sauder did as well, but Sarah was his first priority. Branch could focus on his fugitive.

All Sauder had to do was go inside and tell the guy, this Saul the Saw, that if he wanted the evidence he'd stolen when he disappeared, he had to let Sarah go. Then the two of them would pick up the evidence and do whatever Saul had been ordered to do.

It was risky as hell. But they'd had little time and they couldn't see into the house—the window curtains were all pulled tight—so their options had been limited. Sauder had refused to wear a wire and to be honest Colt didn't consider doing so a very good idea. The first thing this bastard would do was frisk him for a wire. There had been no time for a camera or a microphone to be snaked through a hole into the house as would ordinarily be the case. Firing a flash-bang into the house would likely get Sarah killed since she wouldn't know what to do to protect herself. There were too many variables to play this any other way but the one currently in motion.

Sauder climbed out of the truck and walked up to the front porch. As soon as Colt heard the door open and then close, he moved through the darkness to Sauder's truck. Thank God for all the cloud cover tonight. He'd had no time to change into darker clothes. He'd had to make do with the jeans and blue shirt he was wearing.

Seconds of nothing but the quiet of the night ticked by. He could smell the coming rain in the air. Hopefully this would all be over before that happened.

Shouting echoed beyond the closed door and windows. Saul the Saw was not happy.

Moments later, the back door opened and voices echoed in the night. Sauder's pleading tone and the growling sound of the other man warned that the two would be coming around the end of the house.

Colt hadn't spotted a vehicle. However the man had gotten here, the vehicle was not anywhere close to the house.

Colt braced as the sound of their footsteps told him they were heading for the truck. He was crouched at the tailgate. As long as they didn't come to the back of the vehicle, he was good.

"You drive," he heard Saul the Saw order.

A high-pitched shriek cut through Colt like a knife. They hadn't left Sarah in the house. She was with them. He wasn't completely surprised. Old Saul the Saw would have considered the idea that Sauder was leading him to a trap.

Still, there had been a chance in his excitement over winning that he might have fallen for the first option.

The driver's-side door opened. The truck shifted and then the door closed. Sauder was in the truck.

"Open the door and get in," Saul ordered.

Sarah whimpered and then the passenger door squeaked. The truck shifted again and she cried out.

She was in the truck.

Colt lunged upward and rushed along the passenger side of the truck. He grabbed the so-called

Saw by the hair of the head and jerked him backward. His weapon discharged into the air.

Colt shoved the barrel of his own weapon into the bastard's skull. "Drop it or you're a dead man."

The weapon thudded on the ground.

Wesley Sauder and his wife emerged from the truck, alive and unharmed.

It was over.

As soon as Branch took custody of Saul the Saw from Chicago, Colt breathed a little easier. He pulled out his cell to call Rey and saw he already had a voice mail from her. He walked away from the scene and pressed Play. Her voice whispered in the darkness. She sounded worried or upset. The sound of a car alarm echoing in the background made his heart jump. Then she went on and the fear in her voice twisted inside him.

"Damn it. Call me when you can. I need you, Colt."

He grabbed the nearest deputy and told him to take over for him; he had to get to Rey. Something was wrong, bad wrong.

Thursday, February 28, midnight

IT WAS MIDNIGHT when Colt rolled into the parking lot of the newspaper office. There were official vehicles everywhere. Two city cruisers. Chief of Police Billy Brannigan's truck. The damned coroner's van. Colt's heart rocketed into his throat. What the hell had happened here? He'd tried to call Rey back a dozen times but she hadn't answered. Worry gnawing in his gut, he bolted from his truck and rushed toward the rear entrance.

A Winchester PD uniformed officer was guarding the door. He stepped aside without Colt having to say a word. Good thing; he was in no mood for any territorial nonsense. Inside the newspaper building there were two more uniforms loitering around the lobby. The door to the basement was open and the coroner's assistant, Lucky Ledbetter, was talking on his phone.

As Colt approached the door, Ledbetter ended the call and tucked his phone away. "Hey, Sheriff, I guess you got the news."

Colt shook his head. "I've been at another crime scene. What's going on here?"

"Water main for the building ruptured. The city had to shut off the water to the whole block. Couple of guys from the fire department came over to pump the water out and then Smith Grider started digging up the basement floor to get to the damaged pipes to make the repairs." Ledbetter scratched his head. "It's the craziest thing. They found bones—human bones."

Dread coiled through Colt. "I guess I'll go down and have a look."

"Some creepy stuff for sure, Sheriff."

Colt descended the stairs and took in the scene in the basement. Grider had cracked open the concrete and opened up the ground beneath to expose the water lines. The entire hole was maybe six by ten feet. Burt Johnston stood in the middle of the muddy mess, fishing waders on and holding a human skull in his hands. More bones bobbed in the knee-deep water.

Hells bells. Someone had been buried in this basement? On instinct, he mentally ticked off any longtime missing persons. There wasn't a soul he could think of in his lifetime who had gone missing and remained unaccounted for.

"Colt, you have any idea where Audrey is?"

He looked up at the sound of Chief Brannigan's voice. "Isn't she here?" She had said she was at the paper when she called. Dread gnawed at Colt.

Brannigan shook his head. "She wasn't here when I arrived. She's not answering her phone, either, so Brian went to her house to see if she'd gone home. He said he'd check with the nursing home to make sure nothing had come up with her momma."

Worry twisted a little tighter inside Colt. "What's going on with this?" He hitched his head toward Burt and the bones floating around his waders.

"Don't know. Grider called me as soon as he spotted the skull. Burt is trying to gather up all the pieces." Brannigan assessed Colt for a moment. "You've known Audrey and her family your whole life. Any clue how this could have happened?"

Colt shook his head. "I can't think of anyone who went missing and hasn't turned up. Not in the last thirty-odd years anyway." Colt turned to the coroner. "Burt, you got any ideas on how long these remains have been down here?"

Burt placed the skull on the trace sheet he'd laid out next to the hole. A number of other bones—a rib cage, humerus, femur. Damn.

"Well—" the coroner set his gloved hands on his hips "—considering I recall when Porter Anderson had these pipes replaced the last time— that's when the concrete was poured, by the way." He gestured to the rubble that was concrete and stone. "This floor was originally brick and stone. When the pipes were replaced the last time, concrete was poured over the whole thing to level it up." He frowned. "That was right around the same time Porter died. But these aren't his bones. He was buried over in Franklin Memorial Gardens with the rest of his kin."

"So," Brannigan spoke up, "you're saying the bones have been here maybe twenty-four or twenty-five years?"

Burt nodded. "As close as these bones were to the pipes, they couldn't have been here before the last repair job." Burt nodded toward Grider.

"Smith says his daddy did the previous work and he helped him. Twenty-four years ago next month."

Grider nodded. "We had most of this main portion of the floor dug up. If the bones had been there then we would have seen them. Someone had to put them here right before we poured the concrete. Probably buried them in the dirt around the repaired pipes the night before we poured. Wasn't no other chance to do something like this, as I recall."

Yet that didn't make a lick of sense. Colt asked, "Has the concrete been opened since you and your daddy poured it?"

"No, sir," Grider said with a shake of his head. "This floor was as smooth tonight as the day my daddy floated and troweled it. Besides, if anyone had cracked it open lately it would probably have been me."

Colt and Brannigan exchanged a look. Brannigan doled out the next question. "Did your daddy have anyone working for him who might have had something to do with this?"

"The same four people, including me, have been working for Daddy the past thirty-five years." He shook his head. "Someone had to do this after our crew had gone home for the day. Like I said, probably the night before we poured the concrete."

That didn't leave many options. Colt said, "How

about calling whoever can pull out the file and find out the exact date the concrete was poured?"

Grider reached into his pocket. "I'll call my wife and have her pull the file."

"Thanks." Colt turned back to Brannigan. "We should send someone over to pick up Phillip Anderson and bring him over here."

"Got someone knocking on his door at this very moment," Brannigan assured him.

Hurried footfalls on the stairs had Colt and the chief of police turning in that direction. Colt hoped it was Rey. No such luck. Brian. The man looked worried. Colt's gut clenched.

"Audrey isn't at home and the nursing home hasn't seen her tonight. Her mother is sleeping." Brian looked from one to the other. "I was in such a hurry I didn't notice before, but the passenger-side window in her car is shattered."

Fear put a choke hold on Colt. The memory of the car alarm going off in the background of her voice mail slammed into him. "She was outside when she called me."

The words were no sooner out of his mouth than the three of them were rushing back up the stairs. Outside, Colt was the first one to reach Audrey's car. It was empty. Air finally made it past the lump in his throat.

"Something's wrong." Brian shook his head. "She wouldn't leave in the middle of all this." He turned toward the building. "She was worried sick about the whole mess."

Colt's cell vibrated against his side. He snatched it off his belt and stared at the screen. *Rey.* Thank God. "Rey, where are you?"

"Hello, Sheriff Tanner."

Colt looked from Brian to Brannigan. "Who is this?" he demanded.

"That's not important, Sheriff. The only thing you need to be concerned with are two facts. You have something that belongs to me, and I have something that belongs to you."

"Where is she?" The fear and worry had morphed into something black and menacing. If this bastard hurt Rey...

"You bring Bateman and his evidence to me and I'll give you the woman. Does that work for you?"

"Name the time and place." Colt wasn't taking any chances with Rey's life. Sauder/Bateman was sitting in his lockup at this very moment while Branch interrogated Saul the Saw. He could have him out of there before Branch knew he'd walked through the door. But he knew better than to attempt this on his own.

Emotion was already driving him.

He needed help. And truth be told, there wasn't another lawman he trusted more than Branch.

"I'll call you back in one hour. Be ready to trade, Sheriff, or she dies."

The call ended.

With both Brian and Brannigan demanding answers, Colt put in a call to Branch. When the other man answered, he said, "We need to talk."

Chapter Seventeen

By the time the man told Audrey to pull over, they were just outside Winchester in the historic part of Belvidere at an old gas station that had been closed since she was in college. During the drive she had also concluded that the man was Louis Cicero's son, L.J. He was about the same age as Sauder—Bateman, she reminded herself. He was a little more polished than the two dead guys had been. No need to see the labels to recognize a leather jacket that cost more than the average person made in several months' work. The shoes fell into the same category, hand-tooled leather, probably couture, and the jeans and shirt wouldn't be found in any big-box department stores.

"Get out of the car. Make any sudden moves and I'll put a bullet in your head."

"Whatever you say." She opened the door and climbed out.

He did the same, came around the hood to join

her on the driver's side. "This way." He ushered her toward the gas station.

At the entrance—a plate glass door that was now boarded up, as was the rest of the glass front—he pulled the plywood away from the door and opened it. Inside was black. He dragged the plywood back into place, then used the flashlight app on his phone to move about. He shuffled her into what had once been an office, she presumed, since there was an old metal desk. On the desk was a portable lamp—the sort that looked like a camp light and ran on a battery.

He turned on the light, then used his gun to point to a plastic milk crate in the corner. "Sit."

Audrey did as she was told. He'd already called Colt so help would come. The real question in her mind was how did this guy think he was going to walk away from this? He had no backup as far as she could tell. There was the one weapon in his hand. It was an automatic, a nine-millimeter or a .40-caliber. She hadn't managed a close enough look to say for sure. Either way, he had maybe a dozen or so rounds. Unless he was a dead shot and had several extra clips in one of those high-end pockets, he was screwed.

Not exactly a good position for him or for her.

She should be afraid; she was aware of this as well. But what was the point? Frankly, she had bigger problems. They'd probably found the bones by now. Everything was upside-down. Her mom couldn't remember what happened. Neither Audrey nor her mom was even sure who the dead guy—or what was left of him—was. Maybe the Jack Torrino guy.

Her captor sat on the edge of the desk and checked the time on his Rolex.

"I guess you and your friends were supposed to take care of this for your father. Their failure makes you look bad, huh?"

He assessed her for a long moment. "In my line of work," he said, "you learn to always take out a little insurance to slant the odds in your favor. You are my insurance, Audrey. It took me a couple of days to determine the best insurance policy to go with, but I'm putting my money on you. The good sheriff has a thing for you. He'll do whatever I tell him."

She ignored his attempt to make her afraid. Better men had tried. She opted not to bother telling him that the thing she and Colt had shared burned out a long time ago and had only recently flickered back to life. He might very well be putting all his eggs in the wrong basket.

Instead, she decided a distraction was what she needed. "Did your father send a Jack Torrino to Winchester about twenty-four years ago?"

He puffed out a laugh. "I haven't heard that

name in a hell of a long time." He peered at her. "What the hell do you know about Torrino?"

"You tell me what he was doing in Winchester and I'll tell you where you can find him." Sounded fair enough to her.

He frowned. He wasn't a bad-looking guy. Handsome, actually, in a brooding, self-centered sort of way. "Now why the hell would I care where Torrino is? If he ain't dead, he will be if I find him."

"Like I said," Audrey tossed back, shrugging, "I can tell you exactly where he is. I just want to know why he came to Winchester all those years ago."

"My old man got a wild hair to buy up newspapers. Especially small-town newspapers. He was buying them all over the country. I doubt even he knew exactly what the point was. To look respectable, I suppose. He's always been a little eccentric. Anyway, Torrino was his point man. He did the negotiating with those who didn't feel inclined to sell."

Audrey's heart rate spiked. Like her father. "So he came to provide a little influence in the negotiations on the *Gazette*."

"If he was here, that's most likely why he came."

"Well, that explains a lot." All these years she had wondered what really happened that night and who the stranger was who had been buried in the basement—the dead man she had helped her mom drag down two flights of stairs and bury in the dirt around the plumbing pipes while her father lay dead from a heart attack on his desk.

"So, where is he, assuming you actually know?"

"They just pulled his bones out of a muddy hole in the basement of my newspaper. The one he probably tried to strong-arm my father into selling."

Another of those surprised chuckles erupted out of his mouth. "Your old man killed him?"

"Something like that."

"Couldn't have been you—you would have been just a kid."

She shook her head. "No. I didn't help kill him. I just helped bury him."

He grunted. "Maybe I picked the wrong girl to kidnap. The sheriff might not care if he gets you back."

She shrugged. "You could be right."

He aimed his weapon at her head. "In that case, you're of no value to me."

The air stalled in Audrey's lungs but she didn't flinch, didn't even blink. She would not allow this scumbag to see her fear.

"Except—" he lowered his weapon "—I saw the way he kissed you outside your house. A man kisses a woman like that, he cares. He'll come and he'll bring whatever he has to in order to get you back."

"If I'm lucky." She leaned against the wall and crossed her arms over her chest. "But you know he won't make it easy for you to get away. If I were you I'd cut my losses and head back to Chicago. Two of your guys are dead already. A third is probably in custody if he isn't dead, too. I'm sure your father would be very upset if you ended up that way."

"If I go back empty-handed, he'll kill me himself."

Audrey thought of the story she'd heard about his sister. "The way he did Sophia?"

Fury lit in his dark gaze. "Don't piss me off, lady. Unlike my father, I take no pleasure in watching another human suffer. But I'll do what I have to. My sister made her own choices and she paid the price. I'm not responsible for what happened to her."

Audrey thought about that for a moment. "What about your friend Thomas Bateman? You plan to watch him suffer, don't you? And you will be responsible."

"Thomas made his own choice long ago. I'm just here to clean up the mess he made. What happens to him next is not up to me."

"But you know your father will kill him, maybe

after torturing him. Thomas has children. He has a wife. They count on him."

"He knew what he was doing when he went to the Feds about my family."

"So you do like to watch others suffer."

He stood, moved closer to her, forcing her to tilt her head back as far as possible to maintain eye contact. "Are you trying to annoy me?"

"No. Just stating the facts. I'm a reporter, that's what I do."

He backed up a step, settled onto the desk once more. "Yeah. I looked you up on the internet. You were a hotshot reporter until that jerkoff lied about what he'd really seen in that shack in the woods."

And therein lay the rub. A man had murdered his whole family before turning the gun on himself. Her informant had claimed to be the man's best friend. He alleged he'd been in the room when the murders happened. He'd run, too afraid to face the police after what he'd witnessed. But he'd lied. He hadn't watched a damned thing.

It was a rookie mistake to go with his account even with an impossible deadline.

"Sometimes you screw up. You make a mistake." She held his gaze a moment. "But this is a massive screwup, L.J. You will not walk away from this."

The man was closer to fifty than forty. He couldn't be this shortsighted.

"Let me show you a few things." He grabbed her by the arm and pulled her around behind the desk. "Look under the desk."

She leaned down. There was something under the desk but it was too dark to be certain of what the object was. But every instinct she possessed warned it was an explosive.

"I can't see anything. It's too dark."

He crouched down next to her and turned on the flashlight app again. "See that?"

Her heart stumbled in her chest, then sank to her knees, nearly dragging her down with it. "I see it."

He grabbed her arm and hauled her back to the crate, then pushed her down onto it. He checked his watch again. "In ten minutes I'll call and tell your sheriff where to bring Sauder and the evidence. Once he brings him inside, the whole place goes up in smoke. I'll be waiting just up the road, on that hill, so I can watch the fireworks. One push of the right button and boom! The evidence and Bateman will be history."

"You get to go back home with proof that Daddy can trust you to step into his shoes when he retires."

"You really are starting to annoy me, Ms. Anderson. How about you shut up now?"

She pinched her lips together and watched him

check his Rolex again. He was anxious. Maybe even a little nervous.

A dozen ways to attempt disabling him ran through her brain. She could charge him the next time he checked his watch. She could wait until he made the phone call to Colt and charge him while he was distracted with the call. He was so full of himself that he hadn't bothered to restrain her. She could use that to her advantage. All she had to do was stay alert. React quickly and make whatever she did count.

"Here we go." He stood.

Audrey's heart lunged into her throat.

"Nice meeting you, Audrey Anderson. Too bad it was only for a short time. Hope you've been good, otherwise I'll probably be seeing you in hell one day."

He leveled the weapon at her and the air evacuated her lungs. He backed toward the door. When he stood squarely in the doorway, he flipped a metal latch on the door. *A hasp.* When the door was closed the hasp would fit over the eye loop; the insertion of a padlock would secure the door.

He was going to lock her in.

She pushed to her feet before she realized her brain had given the order to stand.

He shook his head, waved the gun at her. "Sit down and stay calm. You'll have about twenty minutes to contemplate all the things you should have said and done before you die."

One hand dipped into a jacket pocket and pulled out a padlock. He closed the door. She heard the hasp slide onto the eye loop and then the padlock snap shut. Then she heard him talking.

She pressed against the door to hear what he said.

He provided the location and a deadline. Twenty minutes. Colt was to show up for the trade in twenty minutes or she died. He was to bring Bateman and his evidence to this gas station. He would leave Bateman and the evidence inside and walk out with Audrey. As long as they drove away without any trouble all would be good.

Except she and Colt wouldn't be walking out of here any more than Bateman would. They would all be blown to smithereens.

She started to scream his name. As loud as she could, she screamed for him to stay away. When she could no longer hear Cicero talking she understood that he had walked out of the gas station. Now he would go to his lookout position—probably the church at the top of the hill where he'd have a bird's-eye view—and watch. When Colt arrived...

She couldn't let that happen.

He'd told Colt to be here in twenty minutes.

She had to do something to make sure he never set foot in or near this building.

She had to get out.

Pushing with all her strength, she tried to force open the door. Wouldn't budge. No windows. The walls were some sort of wood panels, so there was no kicking her way through.

With no other options, she looked up.

The ceiling was a grid of old dropped ceiling tiles. All she had to do was get up there and she would find a way out of the building via the attic space.

But first she had to get up there. She grabbed the crate she'd been sitting on and stacked it on the desk. Then she climbed up onto the desk and then onto the crate. She could reach the tiles. Stretching, she pushed one out of the way. The grid didn't exactly look particularly sturdy. She needed to be closer to the wall rather than in the center of the room. It made sense that the metal grid would be anchored along the walls. She stepped off the crate and then jumped off the desk.

Holding her breath and praying the explosives wouldn't somehow ignite, she pushed the desk against the wall. She climbed back on top and scooted the crate against the wall and stepped onto it. This time when she moved a tile, she spotted the place where the grid framework mounted to the wall. She reached for it and slowly but surely pulled herself into the attic. It took three attempts and her arms felt like limp noodles by the time she made it, but she was in the attic.

Damn, she should have thought to bring the light. She stared down at the thing. No way was she going back down after it. Pulling herself up here a second time might not be possible. Besides, time was running out. She had no choice but to feel her way around. On one end she could see light filtering in through the attic vent of the building. There wasn't much of a moon tonight. Had to be the streetlamp on that end. She headed in that direction. It was the end opposite the church so the bastard wouldn't be able to see her from his vantage point. Of course she couldn't be sure he would park at the church, but it would give him the best vantage point so she was going with that scenario.

She cut her hand on something metal. She winced. Maybe an electrical box of some sort. Maybe something stored up here. She tried to think when she'd last had a tetanus vaccine. A tetanus shot would be the least of her worries if she didn't make it out of here.

Finally, she reached the end of the building. She sat for a moment to slow the pounding in her chest. Then she took another precious minute to get her bearings. There was no reason for Cicero to be watching this end of the building. He would be watching the road coming from Winchester and the parking lot out front.

With a deep breath, she started pushing on the vent, hoping like hell the nails or screws or whatever was holding it attached to the wood siding were either rusted or broken. She just needed them to give way.

The vent pitched forward. Audrey grabbed on to the edge of the wood siding before she plummeted to the ground the way the vent had. Giving herself another few seconds to steady herself, she calculated the distance to the ground. At least ten to twelve feet. If she lowered her body feetfirst out through the hole, holding on to the bottom of the two-by-four framed opening, her feet would be dangling approximately five or six feet off the ground. She could manage that drop, hopefully without breaking anything.

"Big breath."

She drew in, let it go.

Slowly, she edged out of the hole, allowing her lower body to slip out first. Seconds later she was hanging by her hands. She hoped there was nothing—like a protruding nail—sticking out of the siding or it could rip open her skin, put out an eye.

"Just let go, Rey."

Holding her breath, she relaxed her fingers and her body dropped.

She landed on her feet first and then on her

back. The impact vibrated her bones, made her teeth clack together.

Her head was okay. Neck, she stretched it this way and that; her shoulders, arms, back and legs were okay. No pain, just that freshly jarred sensation. She rolled over onto all fours. If she stood and moved, he might spot her. So she crawled around to the back side of the building. She didn't have her cell so she couldn't call Colt.

If she ran out into the street to try to stop him when he arrived, Cicero would likely shoot at her or at Colt.

"Think, Audrey," she muttered.

If she could make it to the nearest house before Colt arrived, she could borrow a phone. But there couldn't possibly be much time left. He would likely be here any minute. She couldn't take the risk.

There was only one option. She had to find a hiding place and wait until he drove up. Then she'd have to call out to him to drive away.

That could work…if he would listen to her.

Colt Tanner was as hardheaded as she was. Talking him into driving away and leaving her would be like convincing a leopard to change its spots.

Not going to happen.

She needed a better plan.

Colt would be coming from Winchester. There

was only one way into this old part of Belvidere from that direction. He would pass the church before reaching the gas station. She could make her way through the woods, slip around behind the church and onto the other side of the rise. She could catch Colt before he topped the hill and stop him there.

Even as the idea occurred to her she saw headlights coming over the hill beyond the church.

"Damn it." Too late.

She flattened on the broken asphalt and low crawled toward the front corner of the building. Sure enough, it was Colt's truck. He slowed and made the turn into the parking lot.

Her heart thundering, she held perfectly still while he climbed out of the truck and skirted the hood to the passenger side. He opened the door, and a handcuffed Bateman was ushered out of the seat.

"Don't turn around, Colt," she called out in a stage whisper. She prayed he would hear and understand her words. For all she knew the bastard on the hill had binoculars.

Colt stilled. Both hands on Bateman.

"L.J. Cicero is watching. I don't know how many weapons he has but there's a bomb inside the gas station. I was able to get out. When you and Sauder—Bateman go in, he's going to detonate the bomb."

For a few seconds no one moved or said a word.

"Can you run?" Colt asked.

Audrey didn't like the question, but in light of their precarious situation, she answered. "Yes."

"When I count to three I want you and Bateman to run. Run into the darkness. Run fast. I'll call out to you, telling you to stop. Ignore me and just keep running."

"What about you?" Audrey's heart was in her throat. She did not want him hurt.

"I'll be right behind you."

Audrey started to argue but Colt said, "One. Two."

She scrambled to her feet.

"Three."

Bateman ran toward the old general store down the road.

Audrey headed into the woods between the gas station and the old store.

When she was deep enough in the woods she glanced back to see if Colt was behind her the way he'd promised.

Nothing but darkness.

She opened her mouth to shout his name and an explosion knocked her onto her butt.

The sound vibrated the air. The ground shook.

For half a minute she couldn't hear...couldn't breathe.

Finally, she scrambled to her feet. Steadied herself against a tree. Her ears felt as if they were stuffed with cotton. She recognized the feeling. Acoustic trauma.

Where was Colt?

Pop, pop, pop echoed in the distance. The sound was muffled and seemed far away, but she recognized it. *Gunfire.* She started running back the way she'd come. The old gas station was mostly a pile of rubble. Part of the far wall where she'd hidden was still standing.

She ran faster, toward the church. Halfway up the hill Bateman caught up with her. His hands were no longer cuffed. They reached the church parking lot together. Dozens of vehicles descended upon the area at the same time. Blue lights strobed in the darkness.

Where was Colt?

"Colt?"

Cops were everywhere. She spotted Branch. Saw Chief Brannigan.

Where was Colt? Fear tightened in her chest as the sound of all those gunshots fired in her mind. What if he'd been shot? She stared back down the hill at the dust rising from the rubble beneath that lone streetlight.

"Rey!"

The sound of his voice burst through every defense she had built these eighteen long years. She ran to him. Threw her arms around him and held him so tight she was certain he couldn't breathe.

His arms were just as tight around her. "You okay?"

"I am now." She drew back, inspected him in the flashing lights. "Are you hurt?"

"No, ma'am, but I can't say as much for the guy on the ground over there."

Relief rushed through her. She hugged him again. They were okay. They were both okay.

She stilled.

But there was still the matter of the bones.

Chapter Eighteen

Two weeks later

March came in like a lion, as the old saying went. Audrey's life felt as if it had been buffeted again and again by the strong winds heralding spring. The district attorney, Marion Steele, had come to the conclusion that Mary Jo Anderson had shot and killed Jack Torrino in self-defense. The disposing of his body was, however, a different matter altogether. Taking into consideration her dementia, he opted not to pursue the matter, concluding that it would be a waste of the court's time and would not serve any reasonable purpose. In the end, no charges had been levied against Audrey's mom. DA Steele had further decided that she, being a child at the time of the event, was a victim of circumstance and not responsible for the actions that occurred that night. Her uncle Phillip had been cleared. He'd had no idea about the man buried in the basement.

Jack Torrino's remains had been identified and released to his next of kin. Audrey's attorney had spoken to the family and no civil suit was expected. Thankfully, the man whose body had been buried in the basement hadn't left a wife or children behind. Audrey had often wondered if there was a wife or kids who had spent all those years searching for him…missing him, but she had never dared to pursue the idea. Torrino's sister had allayed her worries when she told the attorney that Jack had abandoned his family, her and his brother, when he joined the Cicero crime family.

Audrey stood on the second-story landing of the newspaper and looked out over the lobby, where children from the elementary school were listening to Brian talk about the history of the *Winchester Gazette*. She smiled. This truly was where she belonged now. She had needed time to find herself and to come to terms with the past. She had done both in the last few weeks. She smiled, happy, really happy for the first time in a very long time.

The intercom in her office buzzed and Audrey wandered back to her desk. "Ms. Anderson, there's a call for you on line one."

"Thanks, Tanya."

She picked up the receiver. "Audrey Anderson." Another smile tugged at her lips as she sat down behind the desk that had belonged to her father.

"Audrey! Wow, you are on fire, lady."

Ronald Wisner, her old boss at the *Post*. "Hey, Ron. Thanks for picking up my article on Jack Torrino and the Cicero family." She'd been brutally honest in the article about her and her mother's part in how Torrino met his end. It was time—past time—that secret was fully unearthed.

"How could I not? Louis Jr. spilled his guts and you got the exclusive? How often does that happen?"

"I was in the right place at the right time," Audrey said. She looked around the office. The words were truer than she'd realized when she came home six months ago. This was the right place. The timing was spot-on, as well. She was smarter, stronger. Seeing the world and ferreting out the big stories were enormous accomplishments. But everything led her back home. To put to rest the past...and to be close to her mom.

Now she could relax and just be.

"Well, I wanted to congratulate you and remind you that you always have a place here if you decide to return to DC."

Audrey appreciated the offer. She'd had about a dozen already in the past week. But that was the way of things. One big story could make or break a career. "Thanks, Ron. I'll keep that in mind. For now, I'm very happy right here at home."

Home. She liked the sound of that.

"I hear every publishing house in New York has reached out to get your story. What're they calling it? *Old Bones*?"

"If I decide to do the story, you'll be the first to hear about it."

"An interview would be nice."

After another assurance he would hear from her before anyone else, the call ended. Audrey glanced around at the dozen or so flower arrangements that had been delivered from former colleagues and one very special person. She touched the petals of a pink tulip amid the huge bunch in the glass vase that sat in the center of her desk. The tulips were from Colt. The card reminded her that he owed her a dinner.

She'd meant to call and thank him yesterday when the flowers arrived, but she'd been on her way out the door. Audrey had taken her mom for a ride to see how the trees had budded and bloomed. They'd had a perfect day. Mary Jo hadn't gotten confused or forgotten who Audrey was even once. She'd been her old self. They had spoken about Torrino and how that was over. There was no longer anyone buried in the basement. Audrey had explained how the DA had concluded Mary Jo's actions were in self-defense. The most important part was that her mom had understood. She had nodded and said she was glad that awful nightmare was finally over.

Audrey walked back out onto the landing to watch the children below in the lobby. The tiniest catch of yearning tugged at her. "Let's not get ahead of ourselves, Rey," she chastised.

As if fate wanted to remind her that a child had changed her life forever, Key Tanner came into view. He crouched down next to one of the kids and appeared to explain what the little girl was seeing on the other side of the glass wall. Something about the printing presses. A week ago one of Key's friends had been badly injured in an accident where the teenage driver had been drinking. Everyone had survived and would be okay, but the accident had been a serious wake-up call for Colt's son. He'd apologized to his father and started volunteering for all the projects possible at school to occupy his time rather than partying every available minute.

Audrey was grateful to see the change. Colt wanted his son to be safe and happy. What parent wouldn't?

As he stood, Key glanced up. He spotted Audrey and waved. His smile was so like his father's. Truth be told, he was the spitting image of his father at that age. Audrey waved back.

As many times as Colt had apologized for what happened all those years ago, she understood that he could never regret that beautiful young man currently ushering third graders around the lobby.

She didn't want him to regret his son. Really, what was the point of regretting anything about the decisions they had made in high school, good or bad?

This wasn't high school anymore. It was time to put that part of the past to bed once and for all. One never knew when everything could change. Sarah Sauder likely never expected to be whisked away to some unknown place with a new name and no possibility of ever seeing her father and brothers again. Her life would never be the same, but at least they would all be safe.

Audrey's father's heart had given out on him during the strain of that tragic night twenty-four years ago. Today her mom resided in a memory care unit because her mind was failing her…her brain refused to work logically and accurately. Audrey didn't want to waste a moment more of her life.

A door at the main entrance opened and Colt walked in. He paused just inside and removed his hat, the way a true gentleman would. A smile stretched across her face and her heart thumped a few extra beats. Hat against his chest, Colt looked up, his gaze captured hers, and he smiled.

Inside, Audrey melted. She held on to the railing to prevent running to him. As she watched, he strode across the lobby, pausing only long enough to give his son a nod before climbing the stairs.

Each step closer made breathing a little more difficult. It was foolish, she knew. She was thirty-six years old. He was her first lover, but certainly not her only lover. And yet right now she felt as giddy as a virgin anticipating her first kiss.

"Morning, Rey."

Her pulse reacted to the deep, smooth sound of his voice. She steadied herself. "Morning, Colt." She stared down at the students scurrying around below. "Your son is doing a terrific job with the kids."

"I wish I could take all the credit, but I heard someone visited his school and talked about the growing incidence of tragic accidents among reckless teenagers."

"I might have given some pretty gruesome details in that talk to the senior class."

"I'm glad you did. I could spout the same statistics all day long and he wouldn't listen to me. Coming from you, he paid attention. The whole class was impressed."

Audrey waved off the idea. "That's only because I was on *Good Morning America* day before yesterday."

He grinned. "That might have had something to do with it."

GMA had asked her to do a spot related to the Cicero case. She'd flown up to New York one day and flown back the next. She'd been exhausted when she made it home that night, but she'd had to be up bright and early the next morning for her Career Day chat with the senior class at Winchester High School. The trip hadn't exactly been glamorous, but new online and paper subscriptions for the *Gazette* were up 200 percent. Brian was ecstatic. And the senior class had been duly impressed.

Colt frowned. "I guess you heard the news about Mr. DuPont."

Audrey's shoulders slumped. "I did. How awful for Rowan. And what a loss for the community. Brian's putting together a huge spread in memory of him."

Edward DuPont, the owner of DuPont Funeral Home, had been murdered in his daughter's home up in Nashville, ninety miles north of Winchester. It was a terrible tragedy.

"Billy told me Rowan's coming home to stay. She's taking over the funeral home."

"Really? I hadn't heard that part." Rowan Du-Pont's family had operated that funeral home for several generations, the same as the Andersons had with the newspaper. The paper and the funeral home were started by founders of Winchester. Though she and Rowan had never been close, they clearly had a great deal in common. Winchester was a small town; everyone knew everyone else. Rowan had left for college and made a life for herself in Nashville as Audrey had entered high school. Rowan was a celebrated author and she'd worked with Metro Nashville PD for years as an adviser. Like Audrey, she knew her way around a crime scene.

"My daddy said Rowan and her sister learned how to prep a body for viewing and burial before they were old enough to drive," Colt noted. "I guess it makes sense that she'd want to take over for him now."

"I can understand how she might." Audrey had basically followed in her father's footsteps—even if a little belatedly.

The DuPonts had some very dark tragedies in their history, too. Raven, Rowan's twin sister, had drowned when she was twelve and her mother had committed suicide a few months later. Audrey's friend Sasha Lenoir had a haunted history as well. Sasha's father murdered her mother and then killed himself when Sasha was just a kid. How was it the three of them, Audrey, Sasha and Rowan, could all have such darkness in their pasts and have grown up in the same small town?

Life was strange.

"I was hoping you might be able to take off a little early and go to a late lunch," Colt said, drawing her from the dark thoughts.

She eyed him, feigning suspicion. "How do you know I haven't already had lunch?"

He shrugged. "I might have a source in the paper."

Brian. Audrey laughed. "So he told you I'd been too busy for lunch today, did he?"

"He might have mentioned it."

She shook her head. "Lunch sounds great. Let me get my phone and purse."

Colt followed her into her office. "You know, I was thinking, spring break is coming up next month and the seniors are taking a class trip. I've got a whole slew of vacation days built up and with Key gone..." He shrugged. "Maybe we could get away for a few days."

Colt looked more nervous than she'd seen him since he was fifteen and asked her mom for Audrey's hand in marriage. He'd explained his entire life plan for the two of them to her mom that day.

"Now that's a tempting offer, Sheriff." She moved around to the front of her desk and stared up into his eyes. "If you're sure that's what you want to do."

It was in that moment, staring into his gorgeous gray eyes, that she realized she had just recalled the memory of him informing her mom of his intentions and hadn't even thought about what happened later, when they were seniors. Maybe the past was finally, completely behind her.

And the future was looking brighter all the time.

"I've never been more sure of anything in my life." He tossed his hat onto her desk and took her face in his hands. "I have loved you since I was five years old, Rey, and I want to spend the rest of my life showing you just how much."

Her lips trembled and she wanted to kick herself for being so emotional as a tear slid down her cheek. But she decided she didn't care. "I'm glad to hear it, because I would hate to be in love with you all by myself."

He kissed her and he stopped all too quickly, but the sweetness and the sincerity in that brief kiss were all the assurance she needed to know that they were in this together.

Loud clapping echoed in the lobby.

They jumped apart, remembering the crowd downstairs. Colt's son was clapping. As they watched, Brian joined him. Then the students and their teachers.

Key gave his father a thumbs-up and Audrey relaxed. If they had his son's blessing, they had nothing else in the world to worry about.

"Let's go to lunch." Colt grabbed his hat. "We'll

finish this in my truck someplace where we won't be interrupted." He offered her his hand.

Audrey put her hand in his, ready to follow him toward the rest of their lives.

* * * * *

*Coming next month watch for another
Winchester, Tennessee Thriller,*
In the Dark Woods,
from Debra Webb and Harlequin Intrigue.

*Can't get enough of Winchester, Tennessee?
Read on for a sneak peek at
Debra Webb's new series for MIRA Books,*
The Undertaker's Daughter!
Book one, Secrets the Dead Keep,
coming in May!

Mothers shouldn't die this close to Mother's Day.

Especially mothers whose daughters, despite being grown and having families of their own, still considered Mom to be their best friend. Rowan DuPont had spent the better part of last night consoling the daughters of Geneva Phillips. Geneva had failed to show at church on Sunday morning, and later that same afternoon she wasn't answering her cell. Her youngest daughter had entered her mother's home to check on her and found Geneva deceased in the bathtub.

Now the seventy-two-year-old woman's body waited in refrigeration for Rowan to begin the preparations for her final journey. The viewing wasn't until tomorrow evening so there was no particular rush. The husband of one of the daughters was away on business in London and wouldn't arrive back home until late today. There was time for a short break, which had turned into a morning drive that took Rowan across town and to a place she hadn't visited in better than two decades.

Like death, some things were inevitable. Coming back to this place was one of those things. Perhaps it was the hours spent with the sisters last night that had prompted memories of Rowan's own sister. She and her twin had once been inseparable. Wasn't that generally the way with identical twins?

The breeze shifted, lifting a wisp of hair across her face. Rowan swiped it away and stared out over Tims Ford Lake. The dark, murky waters spread like sprawling arms some thirty-odd miles upstream from the nearby dam, enveloping the treacherous Elk River in its embrace. The water was deep and unforgiving. Even standing on the bank, at least ten feet from the edge, a chill crept up Rowan's spine. She hated this place. Hated the water. The ripples that broke the shadowy surface…the smell of fish and rotting plant life. She hated every little thing about it.

This was the spot where her sister's body had been found.

July 6, twenty-seven years ago. Rowan and her twin sister, Raven, had turned twelve years old that spring. Rowan's gaze lingered on the decaying tree trunk and the cluster of newer branches and overgrowth stretching from the bank into the hungry water where her sister's lifeless body had snagged. The current had dragged her pale, thin body a good distance before depositing her at this spot. It had taken eight hours and twenty-three minutes for the search teams to find her.

Rowan had known her sister was dead before the call had come that Raven had gone missing. Her parents had rushed to help with the search, leaving a neighbor with Rowan. She had stood at her bedroom window watching for their return. The house had felt completely empty and Rowan had understood that her life would never be the same.

No matter that nearly three decades had passed since that sultry summer day; she could still recall the horrifying feel of the final tug, and then the ominous release of her sister's physical presence.

She shifted her gaze from the water to the sky. Last night the temperature had taken an unseasonable plunge. Blackberry winter, the locals called it. Whether it held some glimmer of basis in botany or was merely rooted in folklore, blackberry bushes all over the county were in full bloom. Rowan pulled her sweater tight around her. Though today was the first time she had come to this place since returning home from Nashville, the dark water was never far from her thoughts. How could it be? The lake swelled and withdrew around Winchester like the rhythmic breath of a sleeping giant, at once harmless and menacing.

Rowan had sneaked away to this spot dozens of times after her sister was buried. Other times she had ridden her bike to the cemetery and visited her there or simply sat in Raven's room and stared at the bed where she had once laid her head. But Rowan felt closest to her sister here, near the water that had snatched her life away like the merciless talons of a hawk descending on a fleeing field mouse.

"You should have stayed home," Rowan murmured to herself. The ache, no matter the many years that had passed, twisted in her chest.

She had begged Raven not to go to the party. Her sister had been convinced that Rowan's behavior was nothing more than jealousy since she hadn't been invited. The suggestion hadn't been entirely unjustified, but mostly Rowan had felt a smothering dread, a panic that had bordered on hysteria. She had needed her sister to stay home. Every adolescent instinct she possessed had been screaming and restless with that looming sense of trepidation.

But Raven had ignored her sister's pleas and attended the big barbecue and swim party with her best friend, Tessa Cardwell. Raven DuPont died that day and Rowan had spent all the years since wondering what else she could have done differently to change that outcome.

Nothing. She could not rewrite history any more than she had been able to change her sister's mind.

Rowan exhaled a beleaguered breath. At moments like this she felt exactly as if her life was moving backward. She'd enjoyed a fulfilling career with the Metropolitan Nashville Police Department as an adviser for the special crimes unit. As a psychiatrist, she had found her work immensely satisfying and she had helped to solve numerous homicide cases. But then, not quite two months ago, everything had changed. The one case that Rowan didn't recognize had been happening right in front of her, shattering her life... and sending everything spiraling out of control.

The life she had built in Nashville had been comfortable, with enough intellectual challenge in her career to make it uniquely interesting. Though she had not possessed a gold shield, the detectives in the special crimes unit had valued her opinion and treated her as if she was as much a member of the team as any of them. But that was before... *before* the man she admired and trusted proved to be a serial killer—a killer who had murdered her father and an MNPD officer as well as more than a hundred other victims over the past several decades.

A mere one month, twenty-two days and about fourteen hours ago, esteemed psychiatrist Dr. Julian Addington had emerged from his cloak of secrecy and changed the way the world viewed serial killers. He was the first of his kind: incredibly prolific, cognitively brilliant and innately chameleonlike—able to change his MO at will. Far too clever to hunt among his own patients or social set, he had chosen his victims carefully; always ensuring he or she could never be traced back to him or his life.

Julian had fooled Rowan for the past two decades, and then he'd taken her father, her only remaining family, from her. He'd devastated and humiliated her both personally and professionally.

Anger and loathing churned inside her. He wanted her to suffer. He wanted her to be defeated...to give up. But she would not. Determination solidified inside her. She would not allow him that victory or that level of control over her.

Her gaze drifted out over the water once more. Since her father's death and moving back to Winchester, people had asked her dozens of times why she'd returned to take over the funeral home after all these years. She always gave the same answer: *I'm a DuPont. It's what we do.*

Her father, of course, had always hoped Rowan would do so. It was the DuPont way. The funeral home had been in the family for a hundred and fifty years; the legacy had been passed from one generation to the next time and time again. When she'd graduated from college and chosen to go to medical school and become a psychiatrist rather than return home and take over the family business, Edward DuPont had been devastated. For more than a year after that decision she and her father had been estranged. Now she mourned that lost year with an ache that was soul-deep.

They had reconciled, she reminded herself, and other than the perpetual guilt she felt over not visiting or calling often enough, things had been good between her and her father. Like all else in her life until recently, their relationship had been comfortable. They'd spoken by phone regularly. She missed those chats. He kept her up to speed on who married or moved or passed and she would tell him as much as she could about her latest case. He had loved hearing about her work with Metro. As much as he'd wanted her to take over the family legacy, he had wanted her to be happy more than anything else.

"I miss you, Daddy," she murmured.

Looking back, Rowan deeply regretted having allowed Julian Addington to become a part of her life all those years ago. She had shared her deepest, darkest secrets with him, including her previously strained relationship with her father. She had purged years of pent-up frustrations and anxieties to the bastard, first as his patient and then, later, as a colleague and friend.

Though logic told her otherwise, a part of her

would always feel the weight of responsibility for her father's murder.

Due to her inability to see what Julian was, she could not possibly return to Metro, though they had assured her that there would always be a place for her in the department. How could she dare to pretend some knowledge or insight the detectives themselves did not possess when she had unknowingly been a close friend to one of the most prolific serial killers the world had ever known?

She could not. *This* was her life now.

Would taking over the family business completely assuage the guilt she felt for letting her father down all those years ago? Certainly not. Never. But it was what she had to do. It was her destiny. In truth, she had started to regret her career decision well before her father's murder. Perhaps it was the approaching age milestone of forty or simply a midlife crisis. She had found herself pondering what might have been different if she'd made that choice and regretting, frankly, that she hadn't.

Since she and Raven were old enough to follow the simplest directions, they had been trained to prepare a body for its final journey. By the time they were twelve, they could carry out the necessary steps nearly as well as their father with little or no direction.

Growing up surrounded by death had, of course,

left its mark. Her hyperawareness of death and all its ripples and aftershocks made putting so much stock into a relationship with another human being a less than attractive proposal. Why go out of her way to risk that level of pain in the event that person was lost? And with life came loss. To that end, she would likely never marry or have children. But she had her work and, like her father, she intended to do her very best. Both of them had always been workaholics. Taking care of the dead was a somber albeit important task, particularly for those left behind. The families of the loved ones who passed through the DuPont doors looked to her for support and guidance during their time of sorrow and emotional turmoil.

Speaking of which, she pulled her cell from her pocket and checked the time. She should get back to the funeral home. Mrs. Phillips was waiting. Rowan turned away from the part of her past that still felt fresh despite the passage of time.

Along this part of the shore the landscape was thickly wooded and dense with undergrowth, which was the reason she'd worn her rubber boots and was slowly picking her way back to the road. As she attempted to slide her phone back into her hip pocket a limb snagged her hair. Instinctively she reached up to pull it loose, dropping her cell phone in the process.

"Damn it." Rowan reached down and felt

through the thatch beneath the underbrush. More of her long blond strands caught in the brush. She should have taken the time to pull her hair back in a ponytail as she usually did. She tugged the hair loose, bundled the thick mass into her left hand and then crouched down to dig around with her right in search of her phone. Like most people, she felt utterly lost without the damn thing.

Where the hell had it fallen?

She would have left it in the car except that she never wanted a family member to call the funeral home and reach a machine. With that in mind, she forwarded calls to her cell when she was away. Eventually she hoped to trust her father's new assistant director enough to allow him to handle all incoming calls. Wouldn't have helped this morning, though, since he was on vacation.

New assistant director? She almost laughed at the idea. Woody Holder had been with her father for two years, but Herman Carter had been with him a lifetime before that. She supposed in comparison *new* was a reasonable way of looking at Woody's tenure thus far. Her father had still referred to him as the new guy. Maybe it was his lackadaisical attitude. At forty-five Woody appeared to possess absolutely no ambition and very little motivation. She really should consider finding a new, more dependable assistant director and letting Woody go.

Her fingers raked through the leaves and decaying ground cover until she encountered something cool and hard but not metal or plastic. Definitely not her phone. She stilled, frowned in concentration as her sense of touch attempted to identify the object she couldn't see without sticking her head into the bushes. Not happening. She might have chalked the object up to being a limb or a rock if not for the familiar tingling sensation rushing along every single nerve ending in her body. Her instincts were humming fiercely.

Assuredly not a rock.

Holding her breath, she reached back to the same spot and touched the object again. Her fingers dug into the soft earth around the object and curled instinctively.

Long. Narrow. Cylindrical.

She pulled it from the rich, soft dirt, the thriving moss and the tangle of rotting leaves.

Bone.

She frowned, studied it closely. *Human* bone.

Her pulse tripped into a faster rhythm. She placed the bone aside and reached back in with both hands and carefully scratched away more of the leaves.

Another bone...and then another. Bones that, judging by their condition, had been here for a very long time.

Meticulously sifting through the layers of leaves

and plant life, she discovered that her cell phone had fallen into the rib cage. The *human* rib cage. Her mind racing with questions and conclusions, she cautiously fished out the phone. She took a breath, hit her contacts list and tapped the name of Winchester's chief of police.

When he picked up, rather than hello, she said, "I'm at the lake. There's something here you need to see and it can't wait. Better call Burt and send him in this direction, as well." Burt Johnston was a local veterinarian who had served as the county coroner for as long as Rowan could remember.

Chief of Police William "Billy" Brannigan's first response was "Are *you* okay?"

Billy and Rowan had been friends since grade school. He had made her transition back to life in Winchester so much more bearable. And there was Herman. He was more like an uncle than a mere friend. Eventually she hoped the two of them would stop worrying so much about her. She wasn't that fragile young girl who had left Winchester twenty-odd years ago. Recent events had rocked her, that was true, but she was completely capable of taking care of herself. She had made sure she would never again be vulnerable to anyone.

"I'm fine but someone's not. You should stop worrying about me and get over here, Billy."

"I'm on my way."

She ended the call. There had been no need for her to tell him precisely where she was at the lake. He would know. Rowan DuPont didn't swim, and she never came near the lake unless it was to visit her sister.

Strange, all those times Rowan had come to visit Raven she'd never realized there was someone else here, too.

Get 4 FREE REWARDS!

We'll send you 2 FREE Books plus 2 FREE Mystery Gifts.

Harlequin Presents® books feature a sensational and sophisticated world of international romance where sinfully tempting heroes ignite passion.

FREE
Value Over
$20

Get 4 FREE REWARDS!

We'll send you 2 FREE Books plus 2 FREE Mystery Gifts.

FREE Value Over **$20**

Both the **Romance** and **Suspense** collections feature compelling novels written by many of today's best-selling authors.

YES! Please send me 2 FREE novels from the Essential Romance or Essential Suspense Collection and my 2 FREE gifts (gifts are worth about $10 retail). After receiving them, if I don't wish to receive any more books, I can return the shipping statement marked "cancel." If I don't cancel, I will receive 4 brand-new novels every month and be billed just $6.74 each in the U.S. or $7.24 each in Canada. That's a savings of at least 16% off the cover price. It's quite a bargain! Shipping and handling is just 50¢ per book in the U.S. and 75¢ per book in Canada.* I understand that accepting the 2 free books and gifts places me under no obligation to buy anything. I can always return a shipment and cancel at any time. The free books and gifts are mine to keep no matter what I decide.

Choose one: ☐ **Essential Romance**
(194/394 MDN GMY7)

☐ **Essential Suspense**
(191/391 MDN GMY7)

Name (please print)

Address   Apt. #

City   State/Province   Zip/Postal Code

Mail to the **Reader Service:**
IN U.S.A.: P.O. Box 1341, Buffalo, NY 14240-8531
IN CANADA: P.O. Box 603, Fort Erie, Ontario L2A 5X3

Want to try 2 free books from another series? Call 1-800-873-8635 or visit www.ReaderService.com.

---

*Terms and prices subject to change without notice. Prices do not include sales taxes, which will be charged (if applicable) based on your state or country of residence. Canadian residents will be charged applicable taxes. Offer not valid in Quebec. This offer is limited to one order per household. Books received may not be as shown. Not valid for current subscribers to the Essential Romance or Essential Suspense Collection. All orders subject to approval. Credit or debit balances in a customer's account(s) may be offset by any other outstanding balance owed by or to the customer. Please allow 4 to 6 weeks for delivery. Offer available while quantities last.

Your Privacy—The Reader Service is committed to protecting your privacy. Our Privacy Policy is available online at www.ReaderService.com or upon request from the Reader Service. We make a portion of our mailing list available to reputable third parties that offer products we believe may interest you. If you prefer that we not exchange your name with third parties, or if you wish to clarify or modify your communication preferences, please visit us at www.ReaderService.com/consumerschoice or write to us at Reader Service Preference Service, P.O. Box 9062, Buffalo, NY 14240-9062. Include your complete name and address.

STRS19R